The Scribe

The Scribe

KENNETH STEVEN

CASCADE *Books* · Eugene, Oregon

THE SCRIBE

Cascade Books
An Imprint of Wipf and Stock Publishers
199 W. 8th Ave., Suite 3
Eugene, OR 97401

www.wipfandstock.com

PAPERBACK ISBN: 979-8-3852-5081-3
HARDCOVER ISBN: 979-8-3852-5082-0
EBOOK ISBN: 979-8-3852-5083-7

Cataloguing-in-Publication data:

Names: Steven, Kenneth [author].

Title: The scribe / by Kenneth Steven.

Description: Eugene, OR: Cascade Books, 2025

Identifiers: ISBN 979-8-3852-5081-3 (paperback) | ISBN 979-8-3852-5082-0 (hardcover) | ISBN 979-8-3852-5083-7 (ebook)

Subjects: LCSH: Apocalyptic fiction. | Survival—Fiction. | Regression—Civilization. | Apocalypse in literature. | End of the world in literature. | Global warming fiction.

Classification: PS3563 S74 2025 (print) | PS3563 (ebook)

In gratitude for three American wielders of words:
Wallace Stevens, Cormac McCarthy, and Wendell Berry

When thou tillest the ground, it shall not henceforth yield unto thee her strength; a fugitive and a vagabond shalt thou be in the earth.
Genesis 4:12

I am writing this in a tunnel; at one end of a railway tunnel where there is enough light to see. I am going to fill this notebook with words before the end of my life, and am determined to tell my story before it is too late and the world has gone for good. I am not afraid of trains because there will be no more trains. I do not even know if there are any people left so I cannot know if I should be afraid. I feel like a ghost and I look like a ghost. The only thing I know is that I must write. That is the one thing left to me. I will hold this fragment of a pen in my hand until it is gone. I will hold it like a last candle until it has burned out and its light lost. It is a way of saying goodbye, of singing a kind of song before the end. And tonight I will write until night falls and I am shut into the tunnel with the rats. I will write until their eyes light up red and rabid and they are scuttling over my feet in the darkness. That is all that is left to me, except that I have words. I have the power of story in the pen and story will be my candle. It will light the darkness and for a time it will have a strength that cannot be overcome. I do not know who will find this, who may discover my words. But that is faith; to believe in what cannot be known. The faith to walk into the darkness believing there will be a way. That is what I will do, trusting that what I write will be found and understood. I have come this far that there is no other choice. I must believe and go on believing to the end.

When I was still a child I saw a sign in the underground that asked people to come to the last dawn chorus in the world. It was on a crumpled piece of paper that blew in the filthy wind. I read it many times: over and over again. I was twelve years old. I went that Saturday to the place where we were to meet. I hadn't told my parents I would go there; I slipped out of the flat and went alone. I had a knife in my pocket and I held one hand clenched over that knife the whole time in case I needed to use it. The man who met us had red hair. There were perhaps six of us, no more than that. All frightened and suspicious, as I was. And he led us, at six o'clock in the morning. He was our guide and we followed, though I think that all of us were ready to kill him if we needed to. We had got to a point where we knew nothing. We trusted no one.

I will never forget the tree we came to, with some dead branches. And we stood underneath and the man with the red hair held one finger to his lips so we would listen. We could not see the bird but we could hear it. The sweetness of that singing. We stood there in a kind of circle and listened, underneath the song, as we held weapons ready against the man who had brought us there.

None of us thanked him afterwards. Perhaps even then we feared it might be a trick. We listened until the singing was done and then we melted away, one by one, to leave him standing there, the curious sadness of that half-smile on his face. And yet I believe he was happy all the same; I believe that he was content. He had achieved what he had set out to do and that was enough.

I chose to follow the railway line. I decided that a long time ago. When I was still in the city and living on the seventeenth floor I used to waken up and listen. The bravest thing I did was to get up, to stand shivering in the half-darkness and go to the window. It was a side window, small enough to put my head and shoulders through had I chosen to do so. I bent down instead; I bent down and watched. A long way away I could see the railway line, but I was not watching for trains. I was waiting and watching for foxes. This was their road. They padded in and out of the city by the railway line, making no more sound than ghosts. Orange-red ghosts. If I waited by that window for just half an hour I knew I might see a fox. And that was when I decided. That when I had found the courage it would be the railway line I followed. That would be how I left the city. That would be the safest way, if anything at all might be described as safe anymore. And that railway line and the foxes gave me hope. In a time of no hope they gave me courage enough to put together a rucksack that was filled with the ends of candles, with matches, with a rusty knife, with a bottle of water, and with the book. That is all I have left in the world.

No, that is not quite true. There is the picture of my child, not as she is now but as once she was. The picture of her frozen forever; the way she will always be. But that is not kept in a rucksack full of the melted ends of candles. That is kept next to my heart. For the journey.

↭

The dawn has come and with it the cold. I am sitting almost where I slept and am barely able to hold the pen. The rain is falling beyond the tunnel and it sounds almost like song. I remember being at the cabin in my childhood, listening to the song of the rain and seeing the drops as they patterned the skin of the lake. I was happy to lie like that, doing nothing more than watching and listening. I did not know that the world was about to fall apart.

Now I put out a candle holder to catch rain beyond the tunnel walls. I am afraid of pools of dead water, especially here in the middle of the city. Because that is where I still am: in the middle of the city. All around me are the grey shells of buildings. As the dusk grows they look like eyeless creatures that were turned to stone. They are lifeless and lightless.

There is still the ancient fence on each side of the railway line that separates them from the tracks. It makes this place in the middle a no man's land, and I feel safe here. I have become a fox and I will live as a fox. Whatever might still come out from one of those dead and eyeless stone houses cannot reach me, cannot touch me. I slept in the night without fear: there was no need to waken up and hold my breath and listen. I woke to the gentle choir of the raindrops, and I will wait until there are sufficient for me to drink. Then I will begin to walk at last. I will start to find my path after all this time, having found the courage at last. And there will be no going back again.

↭

Before leaving for ever I looked up and said goodbye to what was my home, our home. All that remains of what was ours on the seventeenth floor. I looked up at the same window from which I looked down, and in that window I left one red petal made of tissue paper. I left it there so I would know the window from the ground. And before I turned away and started to walk through the grey nothingness of the rain, I thought how that building and thousands of others like it are left as nothing more than museums. There are a few pictures of who we were; there are a few boxes of useless things.

They will lie there until time has gnawed at them like rats. And if someone were to come into those rooms they could not put together the fragments of stories they found there. But my child was there; all of us were there, for those last days of our lives in the old world. Yet what evidence do I possess for those days now? They are like stories: they are beautiful and rich and precious to me, but they are not real to anyone else. They are no more than stories, and there is nothing I could do now to prove they happened.

I walked away and I cried a little. My tears washed away by the rain. My grief real and sore and raw until the cold becomes bigger and the rain more important. That is how small we are, how small we become. When everything has been taken from us. The most important thing is where I will sleep tonight. I am not even hungry. I have almost forgotten what it means to be hungry. I see myself sometimes in sheets of water: I catch my reflection and I feel afraid. I hardly know what I have become any more.

I found an old shed; the door of it almost melted away. I could have cried aloud for joy. Inside it smells earthy and damp and the air thick. Once upon a time things must have been stored here for the railway. Now it is big enough for me to sleep in curled up, as a fox would.

That is what came back to me. My birthday was in November but I do not know how old I was. We had gone to the cabin: that was my present, that was the biggest thing I could have been given. The rain whispering on the roof; the apples in the evening. I can taste them still: the cinnamon on the slices and the melted brown sugar. Every room full of the smell of apples; the apples I had picked. And there on the table in the sitting room something wrapped in white paper. I can see everything still as in some painting: the orange-red of the stove window, the white fluttering of the candles, the gold of my father's face as he watched me. And perhaps already then had been planted the seeds of the cancer he did not know he was to carry.

"Open it."

My hands trembling over the paper as they watched me, and I wished to be slow opening it because I wanted to be caught in that moment as long as I could be. The beauty of a moment when there is no time, when you have gone beyond time. Their faces shining as they watched. The deer outside, galloping the autumn darkness in the forest and on the paths by the lake. The warmth of that safe place that showed on no map. That place which was a secret, that had no name except the one we knew it by.

It was a Bible. A Bible bound in brown leather.

∽

It is hard to remember what came first: the marches, the burnings, the election, the violence. All I remember is being afraid: I watched out of a window last thing at night and held my breath because I felt so afraid. If there was silence in the darkness then I believed everything was going to be all right, for that night at least. And I did see terrible things: all of us saw terrible things. But following the thread back to the beginning is the hard part. Going back in my mind and fitting together the pieces of the jigsaw. To know how it all began unravelling. Long before I was born there were all the men from the far right—and they *were* all men. The so-called religious right. I think what came after them in the end was an anger and a rejection of all of that. A desire to rub it out from the page; to make it invisible. To make it as though it had never happened. People were ready for that.

It was the election. Of a man who railed against anyone of faith. It was their fault that we were in the mess we were, and it must never happen again. It must not be allowed to happen. I remember the day I heard the roaring from the stadium. The roaring of his followers. We were to be angry and show our anger. We must not have any more gods interfering in our lives and ruling our countries. We must stamp out superstition and believe in what was real. It was the only answer before us, to rescue us from the mess we were in. And it was a mess that religion had given us. The darkness had come as thousands and tens of thousands were still marching home. I could feel the anger of the streets. That was the coming of Gorwel.

∽

Tonight I do not feel brave. The dark and the cold crowd in on me and I feel afraid. The candle flickers because there is a draught; outside the wind flutters and its breath is cold. I have no idea what time it is. The great clock in the city stopped at six minutes to eight and that is what it will remain for eternity. The thing that was made of time has now become timeless. I miss talking, speaking. I don't even remember the last time I spoke, and now my mouth has grown strange and unused to making words. If I were to speak I would sound like a man who has come in out of terrible cold. I can remember the last real winter there was when we were at the cabin: I have no idea how young I was. I came inside and felt red and breathless: my mother held me close in to her because she said the scent of me was so lovely, the scent of the cold on my skin and the words I made were strange shapes in my mouth; they did not sound as though they were mine at all. I sat by the stove and saw my own breath.

Now there may be no snow left in the world. Perhaps it is here and there in the highest mountains, creeping back a little further every year. All I know is that I will never see it again. Sometimes I dream of it, but only ever of looking in on it. I am looking through a window at what snow must once have been. I am never there; I can never reach it. I can only watch and wish.

Tonight I want to be held. She held me once, before they left and disappeared for ever. She held me and whispered to me and I felt safe, even though nothing could be safe anymore. The world was sliding piece by piece into chaos.

Strange how those things came together: the stadium speeches of Gorwel and my reading of the book, the Bible. That was the book he railed against. It had given us the fools who believed in some literal creation; who believed in a God; who sat in rooms and thought they were talking to God; who could pick up a fossil and think it had been put there to test us. He railed against them until he was beside himself, until he thumped the podium and his voice seemed to carry across the city. These were the fools who had kept us back, who could have acted in time and who did nothing. These were the fools who had chopped down forests and murdered the seas.

I loved the book. Its pages were thin and flimsy. It was already very old. I guessed my father had paid a great deal of money for it, but he never told me where he found it. That did not matter to me. What mattered were the words. I loved the shape of them and the beauty of their sounds. The words of Jesus were in crimson and the rest were in black. I was a child in a time when books were becoming all but forgotten. They had become electronic things that came and went at the pressing of a button. They were not to be held and smelled and touched, not any more. Books had become museums. I heard the voice of Gorwel as I read the book he loathed so much.

Its words were old; they came from a place that did not exist any longer. Many of them I did not properly understand; all I knew was that they were beautiful and I loved them. I lay at night and whispered the words aloud, even as Gorwel lay somewhere else in the city, wondering how to find them and take them away forever.

⟨⊷⟩

Tonight it has cleared completely and there are stars. There is not a breath of wind and the skies are somehow holding their breath. I have the door of the shed open and I am crouched in the entrance, not sitting on the ground because it is so wet, but almost. And I think to myself that my child is up there somewhere, and her mother. Sometimes I find it hard to believe but they are there. I bring out from somewhere next to my heart the remembered picture of my child, of Rayne. The picture does not exist, only in my imaginings. I hold it with trembling hands in the light of the fluttering candle flame. My hands have become like white bones. How much longer have I to live? I do not want to see my face again.

I look at the burst of laughter on her face and at the long rope of her red-gold hair. I remember the moment I wish that picture had been taken. I had wanted her to laugh and I tried to tickle her. As I did I hit my elbow against a table and it was that that made her laugh. She still had that wonderful child's laugh that comes from somewhere so deep inside. It had in it the whole joy of the world. I wanted to take all this away from her. The fear of the next summer; the lawlessness of a world that was going mad. And I could not. Instead she was taken away from me. Forever.

She will always be eight and a half years old to me, until the last day has come. She will always be frozen in my mind in a picture taken on that day when I hit my elbow against a table and the loveliness of her laughter rippled through her. And now I will put the picture back somewhere against my heart. I will blow out the candle and crouch here under the stars and remember her until sleep has carried me away.

⟨⊷⟩

I am following myself back in time. I could not have ended my days in that room on the seventeenth floor. It would have felt like a kind of suicide. I have to do this. The new morning is beautiful and I must move, even

7

though I have the safety and shelter of this shed. Perhaps I am the last person alive, or perhaps there are people just like me in separate corners of the world. I may be the only one with a pen and paper, that is true. Last night I dreamed that Rayne came and found me here. I saw myself lying curled inside the shed, but I was looking at myself from outside. I looked as thin as I know I am. And Rayne came singing to find me. She had brought me a present in a box. She had come down from the sky with a gift and I knew that she was there and I wanted to waken up and find her. The stars were shining in clouds; the skies were so thick with them it was as though a giant had breathed over the blackness.

She had come all that way with her gift and she had known where to find me. But there was nothing that I could do. I lay cocooned in sleep even though I could watch myself lying there from beyond the shed. She looked at me a long time as though she was thinking. Then she left the little box, her gift, beside my sleeping head. She let the door of the shed close and she skipped away, even though the other me, the one outside, was calling her all the time. I wanted her to wait; I wanted her to hear me and know that I knew she was there. But there was nothing that I could do. I woke up and at once remembered the dream. And I wondered what it was that my child had wanted me to have.

I walked on the railway line until I could walk no further. I think that perhaps my mind is beginning to unravel from hunger: I felt I walked all that way with my child, with Rayne. We talked together all the way though I never actually once opened my mouth. She will be forever eight and a half years old to me, and she skipped as she walked beside me. She asked me why it was we had seen no foxes. She said that there should be foxes and that it wasn't right we had seen none, that something had gone badly wrong. And I was not sure what to say to her but I felt just the same that she was right. And then I remembered about the box she had left inside the hut beside me in the night. I asked what was inside and she just answered that I should know, that it shouldn't be difficult to work out.

The railway line was climbing a long low hill and I felt dizzy with the exertion; I was breathless because I was trying to keep up with Rayne. I told her I could not walk too fast and that she had to slow down. She stopped and turned to me and I crouched down for a moment and looked full in her face. She turned her head a little to one side and said that I had to be strong; I must be brave. And she was my child but her voice, her words, were somehow my father's too. And then all of a sudden she started running ahead of me along the railway line towards the top of the incline, and even though I shouted to her to come back she would not stop. The wind came and I shivered with the cold, and when I looked back at the top of the hill and the railway line running into the distance there was nothing. She had gone.

My father was not religious. Neither of my parents were. Perhaps there was something in my mother like a blind hope, the belief that if she did things in the right way, the correct order, everything might be all right. But it was no more than that. My father believed in nothing. He lay dying in bed and I used to think when I went in to talk to him it was as though he had been washed up on a strange shore. He lay always across the bed, stretched out, and his upper body was bare. He was so white. That was what I felt then, that the only change in him was that he became whiter. But there was something wrong with the smell in the room, something I learned to dread. It frightened me. His eyes would find me and somehow they were slower than they had been.

"I can remember the last time the pond was covered with ice. I can remember the last time the song swans came. I waited for them day after day and year after year but they never came again. But that's where you have to go one day. I want you to promise. You have to go to the cabin. I made it with my own hands. I fashioned the wood for it myself and nobody helped me. I wanted it to be for always. You have to go there. This place is finished. You have to take the book with you. This place isn't safe. It won't be long before no one can breathe any more. I wish I could die there. But you have to go back in the end and I want you to take me with you. Please."

I'm just sitting here beside the railway line in the silence but I can remember every word he spoke and the precise order of the words. But I can't remember what I said to him in reply. I wonder if that's what Rayne brought me in the little box. The ashes of my father.

✎

We had an attic in that house, the old house. It was at the top of a flight of stairs and under the roof space. You could go there if you were a grown-up, to do this or that with the piping or to carry down some box that was stored there. But it was not made for grown-ups: it was too low and cramped. It was a place for a child to play and I had games there my parents knew nothing about. I was an only child and I lived in my own head, in another world. I would lie there and dream myself away, just staring. I think now that I was staring into everywhere, not nowhere. It was my place.

There was one window in that attic. It reached out at an angle and you opened it with a long arm, a kind of hook. There were holes in the arm: perhaps three or four of them. And there was some kind of metal hook on the bottom of the window frame so that you could open the window and set the metal arm down onto the hook, either just open and no more, halfway, or fully open. What I liked to do was to stand on a box and open the window as wide as it would go so my whole head could be outside. I felt somehow in the sky; in a whole other world.

And I climbed back there just once years later, during those days when my father lay dying. I went back there on a night when the sky stretched blue and beautiful across the city. I went up there to look, because that was the best view there was. And somehow I managed to stretch my head out of window into the sky. For a time there was nothing but the sky, and that memory of being part of the sky. Then came the sound of the voice of Gorwel, echoing across the night. Robbing my childhood and my innocence for ever.

Take the turbans from their heads and burn them. Take the kippahs and the veils and tear them to shreds. Make a bonfire of their Bibles and let their churches be torn down. For they led us into a mist of superstition, a foolishness we held onto far too long. And their legacy was a broken world. They believed in forgiveness and I believe in retribution. It is time to go out and get even.

✎

What I heard then was a kind of seething. As though creatures with red eyes fled out from that stadium, knowing exactly where they were going. They knew the homes of Jews, they remembered the corner shops that were owned by Muslims, they knew the way that led to every church. And before I brought my head back in to the attic I heard that seething and it frightened me as nothing before had done in all my life. This was the beginning.

"You must hide the book."

I can still remember the sound of my mother's voice. It was as if her words were made of cotton wool, as though the walls were listening. For we could hear the feet out in the street now, though nobody came to hammer on our door. They were going elsewhere, to all the obvious and the easy places. This was long before they began to go deeper, before the madness that Gorwel had unleashed in people buried itself in them so they were listening, so they were watching—everywhere and always.

I didn't know where to hide the book and I sat there uselessly. She got up and went into my room and found it. She swept it up and padded back into the kitchen, expecting me to follow. There was a little storeroom off the kitchen and it had one high cupboard. At the back of it, after you opened a kind of door, there was an inner chamber. That was where she put the book.

"This is where you hide it every time, always. Will you remember?"

I nodded, as though I was somehow still a child. What else could I do but nod? Yet it made me almost as afraid as what I heard pouring from the stadium. It was about the end of liberty. The beginning of the coming of the dark, the coming of the horses.

I had a dream. The most vivid I've ever had in all my life. They came to the house, men in dark clothing who said nothing, just took me away. But I was talking all the time. Telling them they'd taken the wrong person, that I was too young, that I knew nothing. More than anything, I told them I knew nothing. But they did not look at me and they said not a word.

I was taken into a building that looked eyeless. That was what came to me in my dream, that it was eyeless. It was as black and faceless as the men who had come to find me, to take me away. I was taken down black and faceless corridors and somehow I knew what faced me, what would happen next. They would slice bits off me, to find things out. That was what they would do and no one would hear me or come looking for me. And still I was talking all the time, telling them all that I did not know, and had never known, anything and everything. Until we came into that room and I stopped talking at last.

There was nothing there except a typewriter, an old-fashioned machine my father might have found in some antique shop in the city. And it was black and shining, almost as if it was smiling. And they brought me to sit in front of it.

I didn't remember the sound of their voices afterwards, but somehow it must have been the only time they spoke all the same. For they told me that I was the scribe, that I had to write. I had to tell what I had done, what I believed. Then they were gone and I was alone in the black facelessness of the place.

And I sat and typed. At first my fingers were slow, as though not quite understanding what they had to do. But then they grew faster; it was like rain gathering strength and changing from the whisper of a few drops to a thundering.

But I was telling them with every letter and every word that I believed in nothing and that I never had. I confessed that I had the book hidden in secret at home, but that I kept it only because of the beautiful words. And I typed some of them: I hammered them out because I had learned them and remembered them. But I believed in nothing at all: I never had and I never would. No one I knew believed in anything and never had done. They believed in nothing as much as it was possible to do, and I would tell them, I would show them, with every word that I could find and hammer out.

I went on typing and typing, and in the black facelessness of the building there was neither day nor night, just a kind of terrible eternity. Yet when I looked back at the keys of the typewriter from the pages I was typing, I would see that more and more were missing. They must have come and taken them away one by one; the least important ones first, and then eventually the ones that really mattered. To make telling my story harder and harder. To lock me further and further in, until there were only a few words I could write, a few things I could tell. That was the torture I faced.

And then I was awake at last, sitting bolt upright in bed and gasping, my heart thudding in my chest, not sure if I had screamed aloud. And I hoped against hope I had not, so they would not come for me.

⌖

When I reached the top of the incline, the place where I saw Rayne disappearing after she had walked and talked with me all the way up the hill, I stopped to watch. I stood there on the railway tracks, my chest heaving as

I recovered my breath, looking out in every direction ahead of me. How will I have the strength to make it there if I am as pathetically weak as I am now? And how much weaker will I be by then? But she was right: I have to be strong and I have to be brave.

There was nothing, there is nothing. What did I except to see? But that is how we became at the end of the old world, that is what we were reduced to. Poor, sad creatures that were afraid of everything and everyone. We did not trust ourselves any more. Piece by piece we fell apart until there was nothing left. I looked all round, beyond the high fences that bordered the railway line, at buildings that had long since fallen silent. The eeriness of a city that has gone to sleep for ever. Eerier still in the windlessness of that afternoon. But I had reached the top of the hill and beyond where I was standing the line curled round to the right and even descended a little. How pathetic that that should thrill my heart. This is where I have been for the last hour, writing and waiting.

I yearn to find a place to sleep, somewhere I can feel safe and warm, so I can leave fear and nightmare and all of it behind me for one whole night. I have no idea how many miles I still have to go. But I have to do this; I have to make it. And I have to tell this story to the end. Strange I should think still that someone will find it one day. Perhaps that's how we've always stayed alive. By deluding ourselves.

At first we still heard news of things, and then even that began lessening. The bad news started diminishing, disappearing. It was like the slow closing of a door. I think that came home to us a few weeks after Gorwel had given his orders at the stadium. I was out with my mother finding bread for the weekend. And I can remember thinking that she was hurrying all the time; I wondered why she was rushing, why we couldn't slow down.

There was a huge crowd at the square where there was often a Saturday market. She was obviously hoping to find bread. But there were no tables whatsoever to be seen, and she was scurrying about as though determined to find them, with me trying constantly to keep up with her, forever just a few frustrating steps behind.

Then she just stopped dead in her tracks at the back of this crowd of several hundred. There was laughter: two nuns in their habits were being pushed and jostled by a group of men at the centre. They made no sound:

they were like manikins I had seen as a child in a shop window. They put up no resistance as they were knocked this way and that; their faces impassive masks.

Then everything changed. One of the men tore at their clothing and the sound of the tearing rent the air. And there was cheering, from the women and men assembled. Not a single voice of protest. Nor would they break rank to let the nuns escape. More tearing and I caught sight of one of them in just her underwear until that was ripped away too. Then they were standing together naked and terrified in the middle of that throng as the blows and the bricks came in—until they went down, still without a sound.

We came home without any bread. And the news said nothing at all.

Three nights later my father called me out of the night. I woke in the darkness of my room, a long way away in the world of my sleep, and I heard my name called a dozen times and more as I still lay facing the ceiling. At last I got up and went through to the room where he now lay alone, and I saw the whiteness of his face looking at me in the darkness. And he smiled, even though he was in pain. He smiled and told me not to be afraid.

"I want you to read me the creation story."

I went to the cupboard and brought down the Bible. I brought it back to the room and sat down by the edge of the bed to begin searching.

"No, not the Genesis story. I want the verses from the Book of Job."

My hand worked through the Old Testament till at last I found the place.

"Where wast thou when I laid the foundations of the earth? declare, if thou hast understanding. Who hath laid the measures thereof, if thou knowest? or who hath stretched the line upon it? Whereupon are the foundations thereof fastened? or who laid the corner stone thereof; when the morning stars sang together, and all the sons of God shouted for joy? Or who shut up the sea with doors, when it brake forth, as if it had issued out of the womb? When I made the cloud the garment thereof, and thick darkness a swaddlingband for it, and brake up for it my decreed place, and set bars and doors, and said, Hitherto shalt thou come, but no further: and here shall thy proud waves be stayed?"

And when I looked up at last, I saw that he was gone.

I walked down the whole of that incline easily, my heart jubilant. And though she was not with me, I heard Rayne sending out whole torrents of laughter beside me, shrieking as she went. And I smiled as I came down the hill in the railway tracks; I smiled and my mouth felt strange as I did, as it would have felt strange speaking after so much silence. But I was far too slow for my eight-and-a-half-year-old; once she had reached the bottom of the incline she was gone into the distance.

When I'd got there, I stopped to watch, to listen and think. There was just a breath of wind and clouds banked dense and grey on the horizon. There would be rain and with it perhaps a storm. I couldn't remain out in the open overnight, or this might well become my last resting place.

I had been looking at the sky and the next length of the railway line; I hadn't looked for a moment at what lay immediately beside me. And there, almost exactly where Rayne had vanished, was a hole in the wire fence. As though she had brought me here to find it. Beyond, but not far beyond, was a bare brick shed. There was no door at the entrance, and the windows above were nothing more than black eyes in the brickwork. But it was shelter; it was a place to sleep and be out of the rain. I looked about me again as though still expecting someone to be there. I turned right round and there was only the silence and emptiness of a dead world. I went over to the fence, trembling all the same, and took the rucksack from my shoulders. I shoved it first through to the other side. Then I crouched down on my hands and knees, crawled through myself. I was left breathless with the effort; struggled upwards on the other side. And I went towards the shelter.

There was nothing inside but abandonment. Nothing remained but darkness; not even the smell of what it had been was left. Downstairs there was what might once have been a storeroom: up above there were two chambers with bare wooden floors. What I felt almost at once was the rawness of the cold; despite the breeze it was almost warmer outside. I realized the dark would overtake me soon enough and that I had to use what light remained. I left the rucksack and my few pitiful things and clambered down the stone stairs once more. What I needed had to be dry, had to be tinder dry.

I found almost nothing at first: the skeletons of leaves, one of them with such a sharp point that it pierced my thumb. There was the shining of a single bead of blood. I went farther away from the shelter in my search and found nothing more; it was as though I sensed the hunt was going to be useless there. So I came back and went round the walls of the brick building itself. All at once I caught sight of something and bent down to find out what it might be. A small piece of tinder dry wood, shaped once upon a time in some machine room. I guessed it had been something for the line, or part of some box for storage. I was about to struggle to my feet again when I realized that wasn't all, that more lay beneath. Altogether four pieces of dry wood, almost white and weighing next to nothing. If I was lucky, they might burn for an hour in the grate that was in the left-hand part of the upper chamber of the brick building. And now I felt the first drops of rain as the wind began to rise. I had to build a fire before the cold had finished me once and for all.

My mother seemed to age overnight. It was as though she withered, like an apple left on a branch long after the harvest is over. On all those days I thought about the cabin and remembered our summers there. They were my first memories of the world. The drive early in the morning to the place where we had to leave the car. The first view of the lake; seeing the geese on the water, and hearing them as I went to bed that first night. A thrill passed through me that made my heart sing. I lay in that box bed scenting the wood all around me, and I did not want to sleep at all. To sleep would be to waste the wonder of that place, of those days. Instead I sat up and crouched at the tiny window and looked down at the lake. It lay like a light blue gem in the darkness of the trees. In the morning at dawn I would slip out and down to be there, to play on the shore. And there would be deer in the trees; their furry shadows as they folded away into the woods. I was sure I could scent them; catch the lovely musky thickness of their smell. And I would be among the apple trees; I would stretch up and hold whole apples in my hand, and scent their ripe sweetness. Later my mother would give me the special basket and ask me to go down to pick enough for her for the evening. And I would come back with them, breathless and proud, for I had chosen only the best ones. And she would bend down and kiss the top of my head. She would not say a word; just softly kissed the crown of my head.

All that I remembered now, on those days when she aged in front of me. It was as though she was slipping away between my very hands. And it was her mind that slipped away too, as the spring of that year turned to summer.

⋄

That summer began, the one I will never forget. We knew less and less what went on in the city below and around us. Whenever I went out, I locked the door behind me and hurried to do what had to be done and then came home. The heat built in the house. The skies turned strange and metal grey; there was a stillness in the air. It was stifling inside. I went up to the attic and struggled into the little chamber and opened the skylight window as far as it would go: at once I remembered that day and the words of Gorwel. I opened every window wide and I opened doors and I tried to get the house to breathe. And my mother lay in bed, heaving for breath. I remember her eyes; they rolled in her face like those of a frightened horse.

There was one day I went out on some particular errand and I had to cross the main bridge over the river. As always I went quickly, having promised I would be back as soon as I could be. And as I crossed the bridge the stench rose up to me so I had to smother my face before I vomited. I bent forwards to cover my nose and mouth, dizzied with the horror of that stench. But I found myself struggling to the side nevertheless to peer down between the metal slats to the river. But there was no river; the water must have dried completely. Instead there was a sludge composed of mud and plastic and dead fish and seagulls. I gazed at it open-mouthed, my eyes still searching for living water. It had been a big enough river. But there was nothing, only sludge and a dead wave of gasping fish and gulls. It was as though they had been frozen there, as though one single wave of death had risen and this debris had been left forever in its wake. I staggered all the way home, and when I got there I was sick over and over and over again.

⋄

Yet it would not rain and my mother would not die. There was a day I was kneeling by her bed keeping my strange and useless vigil when I thought of the story of Noah. But this version was the original turned on its head: here we were waiting for forty days and forty nights for rain. The ark had on board two of everything that still remained alive: the sea would take us at last to a new land where there would be a new beginning. And a dove would come to the window ledge of her room with a twig in its mouth, a twig that was a promise of that new land. But neither the rain nor the bird came.

I crouched there beside the bed and brought my hand gently over the thin grey hair of her head. And I wished that I could carry her to the cabin, out of the dirt and the bad air and the sadness of the city. But would it be for her sake or for my own? I didn't know if conditions were any better there. Perhaps it would be little more than running away. I had no idea how things were there now; it was long enough since we'd been to the cabin. All I did know was that it was somewhere she had loved; a place she and my father had loved and made together, and that in the end it would be a better place to die.

But there was no safe way to get there, that was the truth of it. I had thought of every possible road to reach the place and discounted each one. The truth was there was no trust left: all of us had retreated into the dark caves of our separate worlds and now watched and waited afraid, our own weapon held and ready. I crouched on and on by my mother's bed as she slipped away a little every hour. Yet one day her eyes fluttered open and she looked at me clearly and surely, her voice no more than the rustle of a bird's wing: "Remember there are apples at the cabin, down in the basement. Don't forget they are there, when the time comes and you have need of them."

I thought about Noah during those days, and the strange voyage of an ark to a new and unblemished land. All of that story was tumbled through what Gorwel had promised at his stadium, that we would search ever more diligently for a new planet for ourselves. The money that might have been spent by right-wing Christians and religious fanatics on teaching a seven-day creation, on schools that were too stupid even to acknowledge science and evolution, that money would be poured now into the search for our new home. And the roars went up from the thousands and the tens of thousands, and I thought of that new home ruled by the voice and the promises of Gorwel.

In the times when my mother slept and her sleep was not troubled, I went to find the book. I brought it out from its hiding place, from the false cupboard, and I carried it carefully as though it was something vulnerable and fragile like a bird. I took it and crouched again beside my mother, and the pages made tiny sounds of crackling as I turned them. I breathed the words aloud as I read them: the stories of Daniel and the lions' den, of Jacob and his ladder of dreams, of David and Bathsheba.

And sometimes now at night there was no power; the city lay in darkness, though that was something else they did not tell us on the news. I rummaged until I found candles that had lain dormant in boxes for years: I went out less and less often until I was almost a recluse. I did not feel hungry; I was glad only of water and more water in the heat of a summer that never came to an end. And I lay awake at night listening to the ticking of my own heart and hearing the breathing of my mother. And at last I would wander through a strange and terrible land of dreams.

When the thunder came in the middle of the night, I went to the window to watch the storm and listen. I felt strangely older: it was as though over the course of the last twelve months I had aged not one but several years. I crouched by the window and at first the lightning was terribly far away: instead it was like some war we were waging away to the east, and the bright glows of the explosions lit up again and now again. By then the heat had become unbearable: the sweat ran from my naked body in rivers. There was silence for a time: no, what there was seemed greater quiet than silence itself. And then the sky was torn in two by the magnitude of the storm, and in the strange confusion of my head I was somehow sure that it was because God was so angry at what we had done. This was the sign of his judgement, of the beginning of retribution.

And then, after the booming and the flickering had gone on for longer than I had ever known thunder and lightning to last, there was something else. It began like a song, and for the first few seconds I had no idea what it was. A song that became a symphony of sound, in the roof tiles and the chimneys and down below in the streets. And then I recognized at last what I had almost forgotten possible again: *the rain*. I opened the window as wide as it would go and I put my head and shoulders into the soft loveliness of that cleansing water. And I cried and the rivers of tears ran down my face and were part of the rain. And suddenly it came to me that this was not God's retribution at all, it was his healing instead. This was a beautiful gift.

I came back into the room in the end and I remembered my mother. I had forgotten her completely. And she was smiling but she breathed no longer. She was gone.

∽

It was the day after my mother's death and I felt strangely liberated. I had no idea what I would do now, far less how I would deal with her body, and yet I felt liberated just the same. I felt what I can only call now the most curious sense of well-being. There was a song that ran through my head.

It was madness, sheer madness. I was a prisoner of my own house and I had barely a sense of what was happening beyond the front door. No, the truth was that I had lost *all* sense of what now lay beyond that door. The only thing I knew was that my parents were both dead and that somehow everything was wrong: the world was being turned upside down.

And yet for that day I did not care about any of that: the faraway skies were filled with strange thin trails of silvery cloud and I thought of dragons. I was a child again at the attic window watching for dragons. It was as though I had tipped over the edge into my own madness. And it came to me that I had not eaten in . . . I barely remembered how long. Yet I wasn't hungry. I looked at myself in the mirror and I laughed at the gaunt face that stared back at me. I was unkempt and wild. But I didn't want to go out. As soon as I thought of that, the happiness within me felt extinguished. And I knew that I was afraid. I was content enough, more than content, within the sanctuary of those walls. More than anything I had a whole world to hide in through the book I had been given. I had beautiful stories, wonderful journeys. What did I need outside when I had such treasure?

Yet recognition that I feared the world beyond the door sobered me nonetheless. I knew that I had to face that world, sooner or later, and I knew that I had a mother who lay dead in the front room. I went to bed that night afraid of the silence and afraid of what I had become. And I realized suddenly that no one could give me answers. I had to find my own, and I had to find them fast.

∽

I know that I took a long time to go to sleep. It was no longer to do with the heat; the worst of those weeks of feverish, breathless, boiling had been broken by the coming of the thunder. It was nothing but the turmoil of my own head. I simply did not know what to do next. In the end I must have wandered into sleep, but it was as though I padded a land that lay somewhere in between. I think I dreamed of long corridors that extended behind the house. I walked them endlessly, searching for something and never knowing for sure what it was I sought.

There was a noise, a hammering that went on and on, and for a time I was still somewhere in those corridors, wandering, not sure where it was the noise was coming from. Then I opened my eyes as I lay on my back in the bed, and I heard the thundering on the door at the bottom of the stairs. The outer door. I lay rigid, barely able to breathe. And the hammering came again, still more urgent.

I got out of bed in the pitch darkness, my chest thudding, and I reached for the light switch. There was nothing. I pulled on clothes that had not been washed for as long as I could remember, and I scrabbled on the table to find the torch that still held a precious bit of life. I staggered downstairs as the hammering came again and I heard my voice asking terrified who was there, what they wanted. And I stood there, unprotected, clutching myself, in front of the door.

"I need to come in. My name's Lisa and I have a child."

I have no idea if it was that knowledge that made up my mind. Whether it was or not, I found myself opening the front door at four in the morning. I was unarmed, in a world that had fallen headfirst into madness.

I was able to build a fire in the grate of the upper chamber in the end, but my fingers had almost forgotten how to work by the time it was done. It had always been my task to light the stove at the cabin and I loved it. I learned to find the right kindling; I knew where the driest sticks were to be found, and the best. I brought them back and built something in the stove that never failed to light with the first match. My father used to smile at that; he was ever amused by the challenge I had set for myself. Little did either of us know that I was serving a kind of apprenticeship. Because now I had thirty-four matches left, and what would I do to make fire once they were gone? Tonight I had to use two because the draught caught the first match and extinguished it. The second had to be the one that worked: I could not afford to waste any more.

What I did realize almost as soon as I came back to my brick shelter was that the wood I had found was uselessly little. It would last me nothing like an hour. So, long before I had used my second match to light the fire I went back into the gathering dusk. The rain had all but passed now; it was the kind of shower that won't quite finish and I kept waiting for the last heavy drops on the roof to cease.

In the end I knew I had to go back out before the dark fell completely and any search would be useless. How little can we predict what will happen. Outside I found not a shred more timber, but my eyes happened to fall on a patch of growth along the back wall of the building. I knew it from childhood: sorrel. I used to pick the leaves to suck when I was playing by the shore of the lake. They tasted of lemon and were full of goodness. Back then I ate them simply because I thought they tasted good. I clawed at them now: picked perhaps fifty or more to take back upstairs with me. Before the rain returned.

But just as I was about to go upstairs again, I caught sight of something at the back of the lower chamber of the building. My hands were full of sorrel leaves so I carried them up first before returning to find out what I had glimpsed. I felt dizzy climbing the stairs: at least I would have something by way of sustenance before I slept that night, and a little more in the morning. When I came back down and started out across the stone floor to find out what I had seen in the shadows, I knew before I got there that someone had been here. My feet kicked a pile of what I was all but certain must be bones: I did not need to make sure by starting to search with my hands.

But what I had caught sight of from the door lay beyond: a small box with pieces of wood inside, perhaps twenty in all. I crouched there and began to work out what must have happened: someone had sheltered here with their precious box, hoping to build a fire. Perhaps they had died before they even got that far. I had seen too much and I had come a long way from the child who had once gone out to find wood for the stove at the cabin. But whatever exactly had taken place, I was sure a pitiful life had ended in this place. I whispered some words from the book, so much of which was written inside me now, and though they felt useless and small words, I wanted to whisper them just the same because they were beautiful. And I thanked that pitiful soul for the box of wood they had left there.

22

And of course after however long hidden in the corner of this place the pieces of wood were perfectly dry. I crouched there by the flames, my face caressed by the warmth. And I ate my first food in days: twenty-six leaves of sorrel. And before I slept that night, I set out my cup in the darkness beyond the doorway below for any rain that might fall before morning.

⌐⌐

I looked at the girl called Lisa, out in the darkness, the child in her arms. I must have looked at her as though I had never set eyes on another human soul before. She pulled the child higher onto her hip and looked around her where she stood on the step.

"Well, you'd better decide if you're going to let us in or not. She might not make it through the night otherwise. It's up to you."

I still said nothing, but I gave my answer by standing to one side and letting her climb the stairs. I had nothing here to offer them. My dead mother still lay in the front room. But there had been little choice. The girl called Lisa stood in the upper hall and waited for me, almost as if it was me that was coming in.

"She hasn't slept for well-nigh forty hours. I need a bed for her and I need water. I don't care about myself but I have to see right by her."

It was as though the place was not my own, as though I had forgotten where things were kept or how to do anything. It was the strangest moment in the midst of the strangest time. The child clung to her as a young animal might cling to its mother: the big eyes searched around her, taking everything in. Then the child started whimpering.

"You make any crying and you're in trouble, you hear me? You'll be asleep in half an hour, but I have to wash your cut first. If I don't do that it'll be sore all right. Then you'll have something to cry about, I tell you. Now stand there quiet and I'll wash it for you."

I had put a candle in the bathroom. And I remember watching the two of them from behind, the woman bent over the child. And what I remember more than anything was the tenderness of her hands. Then I went to start getting a bed ready for the child.

"We've been two days wandering. I've held her for most of that time, and she's hardly light, despite not having eaten properly for however long, poor mite. It feels like the whole city's on the move. Why? How long have you got for all the reasons? Hunger, illness, confusion. I don't know. There hasn't been a sign of Gorwel for God knows how long. Someone's probably done away with him: didn't like what he said, or else was too scared by it. Whatever he had, the man had courage. And I don't care what anyone says. So what're you doing here? What's your story?"

I told her about my dead mother, how she had died not long after my father. I gave her some sense of how long we had been here. She stared at me, snatched up another of the biscuits I had found in an old tin. There was more shouting out on the street: the sound of breaking glass.

"You're not used to bodies, are you? I'll bury her for you. That much I can do. As long as you watch Rayne. That's the only thing that has to happen. And then you need to go and find things."

I swallowed, asked her what she meant, what she was thinking of.

"Bread, vegetables, anything edible you can lay your hands on. You can forget any hope of milk; that's long gone. I don't think you have the first idea how bad things are, or how bad they're going to get. And this place is too near the ground. We should be higher up. Further away."

I nodded, understanding. It felt good when she said "we" like that. I went through to the kitchen and rummaged through every tin, found one more biscuit which was pretty much stale. And I brought back another candle, as the one I had lit when they first arrived was about finished. I passed the hiding place of the book when I came back. I was already wondering what I would do about that. It was my secret and mine alone.

We looked in on the child and she lay curled like a doll, fast asleep. Lisa tucked the duvet round her and quickly turned away.

"I'll come in and sleep with her later. We'll be fine here. She'll sleep till kingdom come, poor mite. She's seen things no child ever should."

We went back into the other room and sat down close to the candle. I asked her what she thought would happen now. She did not look at me, just breathed out a long time and shrugged her shoulders.

"You'll get a sense of things as soon as you go out tomorrow, when you have to go out. Everything's happening fast. There are factions. Whatever anyone says about Gorwel, he wanted to keep things together. Maybe he was naive about that, I don't know. Once you take things from people the glue's gone. You can't hold a country together without heat and light. A hell of a lot of people. Old and young and in the middle. It was forty-five degrees. No one knows what's going to happen and they're scared. All we are is animals with electricity; that's what my mother used to say. But the word is they've found the planet they were looking for. It may be they knew about it the whole time and simply never told the people. I mean the old lot, way before when Gorwel came on the scene. That's what I'm holding out for. That's the only chance we have."

It was five in the morning and there was the beginning of greyness in the skies. She was beyond tired herself and I wished her a good night.

"There'll be nothing good about it. It's just about forgetting. There's nothing good about what we have left here, that's the one thing I know for certain."

Last night I was warm in this brick shelter. The wood gathered by a dead man burned well, just as I knew it would. But I had to creep in as close to the flames as I dared; whenever I went any distance away it was cold as the grave. The place is just brick walls with empty windows and no door. I got up at whatever time through the night to look out over the city, make sure there were no lights. It is that fear someone might be waiting, watching—even now. I am haunted by the need to know, be sure. I went to the window while the final bit of the last piece of wood was burning, just before I lay down to sleep. Nothing. Not so much as a glimmer of light. Silence. The sky had cleared again and the stars were up like a sparkling of frost; I can remember my father telling me the dead ones were those that shone like that. We should be the same: a warning to anyone watching somewhere out there.

I found it hard to find a comfortable way to sleep. I wanted to be close to the last glow of the fire but the floor felt so hard underneath me. And the cold came up through that stone floor like ghosts. I was thinking of whoever it was that gathered the wood I burned tonight, the person who must once have died down there. Cold is the kindest killer, that's what they say. May it have been the cold. We haunt our own darkness, though. There was nothing outside and the possibility of nothing; I had seen that from the empty window. And yet I lay listening for the sound of footsteps like some five-year-old child. In the end I slept sitting up in the corner, with my back against the wall. It was the only comfortable position I could find. I wanted to dream of Rayne, but I dreamed instead of someone I didn't know coming up the stairs to watch me.

In the morning it felt as though someone had poured lead into my arms and legs. I had slept in the end, though never deeply, probably for four or five hours. The pain of moving now was hellish. I said things in that empty brick room I have never said before. Not just about pain, about the whole misery of existence I have left to me now. I am on a journey I may well never finish. Perhaps it would be better if I fell asleep one night and never woke up. Yet I cannot bear the thought that I end up like that wretch who died with their pitiful fragments of wood. What else can I do but rail against the pain of the darkness? Yet it has to be about more than that. I have to find a purpose somewhere at the end of this journey. I do not want to die without finding some kind of light.

After half an hour of chafing my arms and legs in the upper chamber of this place I felt stronger and the pain had passed. And it was a better day, though I saw that it must have rained in the night. That meant it must have been raining while I was sleeping, for I had heard nothing at all. That reminded me of the container and I went over to the steps to descend. I almost howled with the pain of that first step down; I took it much too fast. I went down the rest of the steps like some old man on crutches. But when I finally made it to the bottom and went outside I found the tiny candle holder full of crystal clear water. There might be all manner of chemicals in it from a damaged sky, but it is too late to worry about such things. I bent down for it with gratitude and went back up the stairs, slowly and carefully.

I crouched by the remains of the fire and I drank that water and ate another twenty-six sorrel leaves. I resolved that I would stay here another night and build my strength before going on. It was too good a shelter to leave quickly. I had the whole day to search for more wood. And I had the whole day to write.

✑

"Waken up. You need to get out there as soon as you can. And not just for food."

The voice by the door startled me. I sat up, covering my nakedness.

"I wouldn't worry about that; I couldn't care less. But I'm worried about the child. The cut she's got's gone bad; it's all coloured round the edges. So as well as finding food you've got to try to find a doctor."

The room was still shrouded in grey: I knew it couldn't be more than seven in the morning, if it was as late as that. I scrabbled to find my clothes.

"And you'll need some kind of weapon. You're not having mine because I don't know who might try to break in here when you're gone. Best take a knife: that's going to be easiest to carry and it scares them most. But don't even think of risking going out there without protection. The world's changed since you were last outside, let me tell you."

With that Lisa disappeared. I heard her talking to the child in the next room. I could hear the sleepiness of the child's voice. The whole of what had happened through the night came back to me now in fragments, and fitted together in the end to become a single story. I thought of how afraid I had been of going out before I knew any of what had happened, before I was even half aware of how things had fallen apart. And Lisa had hardly saved me from the worst of it, that much I guessed. But going out was not a choice any longer; very little felt a choice any more. All at once she was back.

"Oh, and you need a knife rather than money. If you're lucky enough to find a shop that's left intact and that's got supplies, then please and thank you and the right change don't work anymore. All you have to do is grab and go."

She was quiet a moment and hesitated, before turning back to the door.

"If it's safe, I'll see to your mother and I'll do it with dignity. I just hope you can find a doctor—it's not exactly going to be easy. And take care out there."

✑

What got to me first more than anything else was the silence. A city is the place that never sleeps: the slush of traffic, the echo of voices, the sound of feet. This was a city that had gone into hiding. It was as though it was holding its breath. I felt as though eyes might be watching me from seventh-floor windows. I heard the rattling of something as it was carried along the gutter in nothing more than a breath of wind. And I smelled . . . something. The air was bad, felt almost difficult to breathe. I stood there for that first moment, not sure how to move, far less where to go. I had shown Lisa everything: she had locked the door behind me and would recognize the secret sign I gave on my return. And there was no way I could come back empty-handed.

But the fear I felt only mounted in those first moments. I shrank back into the side passage which led to our square of garden and our shed. I sank against the wall and held the knife so hard in my pocket I felt the pounding of my heart in my forefinger and thumb. And then the words came into my head.

"The LORD is my shepherd, I shall not want. He maketh me to lie down in green pastures: he leadeth me beside the still waters. He restoreth my soul: he leadeth me in the paths of righteousness for his name's sake. Yea, though I walk through the valley of the shadow of death, I will fear no evil: for thou art with me; thy rod and thy staff they comfort me."

That was sufficient, and I did not even breathe the words, I only thought them, saw them in front of me. I knew where I would go: I suddenly realized what might be possible. If I could reach that far in safety, but this was what I had to believe. The first fear had passed. I had to do this first and foremost for a child, not myself. I emerged from my place of hiding, walked back the way I had come, and immediately turned out onto the road.

I changed my mind. I knew I had to leave the brick shelter while the weather held: the longer I stayed there the less I would want to move on. I ate all the sorrel leaves I had gathered and saw there was precious little in the way of kindling or more substantial wood to make another fire anyway. I would have to pick up the fragments I found along the way. As I came down the staircase a last time I felt the memory of that soul in the ground-floor chamber of the brick building. That was who had come to look at me the previous night. That was who would come again this night if I were to remain. Better truly to sleep in the open than above the sadness of that death.

But I was not fool enough not to stop and pick every last sorrel leaf I could find. I counted another thirty-six leaves: I would eke them out.

For all the apparent abandonment of the city, I preferred to return to the railway line to walk. It came to me that I still had not seen a single fox, and I wondered if they were all dead too. It would have been strangely comforting to see one now; it would have made me feel less wholly alone in this world. And yet I kept looking round for things that were not there: I hadn't come to terms with the emptiness, not even yet.

I could not make up my mind about the day. There was the tug of a wind, and heavy clouds to the north and west, but the skies were bright enough above me. What was without doubt was that I felt far stronger: more alert, more ready and able to walk. I was thankful for that brick shelter but glad enough to leave and move on just the same. I only wondered now for how long I should follow the railway line. The time had to come when I struck out into the woods, but I knew I wanted to leave that moment as long as possible. Perhaps that too was little more than the fear of ghosts, but the truth was I didn't know for sure. I followed the railway line: straight and sure into the west.

So I left the shelter and the safety of the passage and went out onto the street. What did I expect? To see faces watching from windows? To be cornered at once and challenged or attacked? None of these things happened, but I felt the faces at the windows all the same. I was not fool enough to look up and around me and to do so with apparent fear, but I felt those faces all the same. I had learned to be wise enough in a city of several million; I had street sense, however much that counted now in a wider world that had lost all sense of reason, that had most likely grown paranoid. There was the key: at the heart of everything lay fear. And the evidence was visible on every side.

I knew exactly where it was that I wanted to go, even though I had no idea if it still existed. But I had to believe, and I walked at the very edge of the pavement, keeping as perfectly straight a line as I could. And I kept my head down, literally, though not so much that I could not see what was around me in the street. There was a torn book lying in the gutter. I guessed at once as I passed it that it must have been a holy book of some kind. And there on the other side of the street, on the white wall, was a grotesque caricature of a Jew as a pig with little round glasses, daubed with black paint. And further on still there was what I had no doubt was blood, and worse, though I did not have the courage to look more closely. But all I heard was the soft sound of my own footsteps, and the sound of my heart in my head, for I felt far from unafraid. Then I reached the end of the street and turned up the little alley to the left. I had made it this far, though it did not mean for an instant I was now in greater safety. The smaller lane would be every bit as risky as the bigger street I had left, but I felt I had accomplished something nonetheless. And now I was nearly there.

⌀

And as I passed into the tiny alley and glanced in to my left, to what had been a shop front through all my early childhood, I caught the flicker of a face. It was a face I recognized and knew, though I had not had the chance to show that recognition before the face had disappeared. But I simply stood outside that old door I had come to know so well, as though I was still twelve years old and nothing had happened. And all at once like a wave coming over me I remembered the morning I had gone to what had been called the last dawn chorus in the world.

At just after nine in the morning I had come for a bag of sweets and I had sat in the dark shadows of the shop and talked to Mr and Mrs Newman, for they had no children of their own and they were never in too much of a hurry not to offer a welcome. And I remembered sitting and telling them the strange story of what I had experienced.

I stood there now, smiling as though I was still twelve years old and as if nothing at all had changed. And since that day the world had been turned upside down.

The door opened suddenly, though only sufficient for Mrs Newman to half-drag me inside and clatter the door shut and lock it behind me. She pulled me through into the front room with its faded posters and tumbling of scents. She looked as though she had aged twenty years.

"If I hadn't seen your face as you turned the corner I would never have let you in. What is it that you want? I don't have much time."

"I am looking after a sick child, Mrs Newman. I am sorry if I frightened you. I did not know where else to go. If you have even a little food for the child, and perhaps plasters for her wound? That is what matters most."

She looked at me from the shadows of the room and made up her mind.

"Come upstairs with me then and I'll find whatever I can for you."

↤

In the end she gave me far more than I had asked for. I refused to take all the plasters, persuading her she might yet have need of them herself. She gave me a tube of ointment that looked incredibly old, but she swore it would only do the child good. There was a little pair of gloves she made me take, even though we were enduring the hottest summer in history. She had knitted them once upon a time for her niece and for one reason or another had never given them to her. Then she bustled downstairs once more and I tramped after her on the narrow staircase. It felt almost eerie being back there: half-forgotten memories of the place and of things that had been said were tumbling through my head.

She gave me all the food she could spare; last of all three pieces of cake that she wrapped with such care in a crumpled sheet of foil.

"Arnold would've wanted me to do all this."

She said the words and did not look at me, but busied herself putting everything in a bag. I knew Arnold must have been her husband, and I searched for the words that I wanted to speak and felt suddenly twelve years old once more.

"He died before Gorwel came to power and I thank God he did. I don't want to be alive without him but I was here for you today and that was meant to be. One more thing I want to find for the child . . . ."

She bustled away and returned in a minute or so with a paper bag twisted in her right hand. I knew what it was at once. She found a place for it in the bigger bag.

"Sweets for the child," she breathed. "For when she's better," and she smiled.

I leaned forwards and hugged her a moment. She pressed me to her very quickly and then let me go. I could see the glittering of her eyes.

"One last thing, Mrs Newman. Have you any idea where I would find a doctor?"

She thought, then found a pen and wrote something on a scrap of paper.

"I don't know if he's still there, but you can try. Say that I sent you."

I went out and this time it was worse, for I had no real idea where I was going. I thought about all the tablets and the gadgets we had had: every one of them useless now. They were shining black screens that were speechless now, that had nothing more to say, their maps and directions forgotten. I was already thinking where I would go, where I would stop and plan. I prayed there might be no one in the street down which I had walked in the other direction.

But there was one man, sitting in a doorway about thirty yards ahead. I thought of turning round and returning the way I had come, but I remembered the rule I was trying to learn to obey: *Keep going straight ahead. Show no sign of fear and do not give anything away by the expression on your face or by your walking.*

Already I could hear the man talking, pouring out an unending torrent of words I still could not make out. I would pass within a yard or so of where he lay crouched in the doorway.

I would not look at him. I would give no sign that I had heard him. Now his words were becoming audible as I stepped closer and closer to his hiding place.

"Please, if you have anything at all, I beg you. I'm not asking for money but food or water. Have a heart and help a man save his life!"

I broke my own rule to myself and glanced just and no more to my left as I approached. Perhaps it was for the best. He was wearing a long coat and one hand was hidden inside. I caught the flash of the edge of the knife as I passed.

My heart hammered. What if he was enraged and got up and pursued me? I quickened my pace even though I kept telling myself not to.

"You bastard! You filthy bastard that you could spare nothing! Was it too much to ask for one morsel of bread?"

I reached the side street where our flat was. I went back into the lane and bent forwards in gratitude and relief.

Then I realized what the best thing would be to do. I had food for the child and something in the way of medicine: I'd go back with them now to the flat.

I breathed deeply and went out from the side alley. I raised my clenched hand to the door to give Lisa the knock we had worked out. And I held my breath.

"How long have you been gone and you come back here without a doctor? Rayne's a lot worse than she was and that's all you've got with you? I'd have been better off going out there on my own. Come and see her for yourself!"

I knelt down beside the bed while Lisa thumped things down in the kitchen and went on ranting to herself. I smiled at the little girl and she smiled back, a little afraid. There was a smell in the room, something that wasn't right. I whispered a few words to Rayne and held her hand. Then I put the little bag of sweets into that hand and put a finger to my lips. I smiled conspiratorially to her and she understood my meaning at once. But I knew that Lisa was right all the same: next time I had to come back with a doctor.

I went out of the bedroom and into the kitchen. My voice was quiet.

"Do you know where Marron Street is? That is where I have to go. And I could not exactly stop the first person I met to ask them directions."

She said nothing to that but it was clear the tirade was over. I could see she was thinking, trying to remember. She went over to the window, looked out.

"I'm not sure. I didn't grow up in the city like you. I think it's up that way, whatever direction that is. But I can't be certain my memory's right."

I smiled in sudden triumph. I had remembered the box in the attic.

"We have old maps. Real maps. I'll work out my route from one of them."

I have been writing for I do not know how long beside the railway line. I am somehow more there than here: more in the memory of all that took place over those days than I am in this dead no man's land. Nothing has happened to me for so long now: my whole existence is poured into the pages of a book where I re-live every word and movement. But the place where I am seems to sum up all the reason for the silence: on the far side of the railway tracks, just beyond the high fence, are four metal drums, taller than I am. One of them has toppled over and from the opening there is trickling a long thick trail of green-blue liquid. All the ground around it is dead, completely dead. The plant life has turned a grey colour, as though it has somehow grown old. And I feel it is a kind of metaphor for what humanity did to itself in the end. There was a poisoning of the seas, the forests, the earth itself. Except that, in the end, the poison had to be drunk by the one who was doing the poisoning. That was the price to be paid.

And then I turn round and my eyes scan the miles of empty homes, the dead cars, the silent schools. I think of that poem by Shelley of the great sculpted figure in the desert, and the lone and level sands stretching away around the nothingness of what came afterwards. If this book survives, then perhaps it can be a warning. That is what I hope. But perhaps it is simply too late. I know what I want to do with it and I am determined to fulfil that before I die. I have a long way to go, in every sense. It is the silence that haunts me. We were not meant to be alone and I have been alone too long. I will be alone at the end too, I know that. I can only hope that I see the faces about me then, that they are with me as I sink into the closing of the light and that I hear their voices. I can have no greater hope than that.

I found the map I had remembered in the attic, thanked God my father had not thrown it out. But it had been saved by his stubborn love of everything old. He was not impressed by a map you could move and see in different ways at the touch of a button. It was for the same reason he had given me the Bible for my birthday. Not only for the love of words but because of the very scent of the paper, the sound of the pages as they were turned. All those elements were bound together, could not be parted from each other. And so I brought it down, the map of a city that was so old it had all but fallen to pieces.

Lisa made space for it in the kitchen on the table. Her voice was low.

"Rayne is fast asleep. It might do her good, poor mite. Once you're back and I can worry a bit less, I'll see to your mother. I've not forgotten. I'm grateful for what you're doing. I know I may not show it but I'm grateful."

We looked together at the map; found where we were and worked out the route. I took the scrap of paper Mrs Newman had given me and I turned it over. I followed the route on the map until it was imprinted in my memory. But I wrote out the order of the streets I had to follow just the same. It was unknown territory. I realized how solitary my growing up had been. I did not truly know my own city. But it had not been a lonely growing up, rather a solitary one—and there was a difference. My best friend had been the attic. I had spent hours and days and weeks up there, as much as anything living in my own head. Until the day that spell was broken by the speech of Gorwel and something was shattered. It poisoned the place; left the air strange to breathe.

"I have no idea how long I will be," I said. "All I can promise is that I will be back the moment I can be. I cannot even know for sure I will find this doctor."

"I understand. I know that." She paused, then her eyes glittered as she closed the door on me.

⌭

Already it was growing hot. There was not so much as a breath of wind in the city and the skies were as they had been on the night when Lisa and Rayne first arrived—grey and somehow made of metal. I was glad I had had the presence of mind to come back first with those precious few mouthfuls of food for the child or they would have been soured in no time in the heat.

The question was how to move. I was learning all the time. I knew that I had to stop for nothing and for no one. Had I gone to help that beggar in his doorway I would have been knifed and left for dead. I walked now in the middle of the street: from there I had the best vantage of what might lie ahead, and I was away from windows. I remembered what I had read about a dissident way back in the days of the Soviet Union; he had been on every wanted list there was. And in the middle of winter he had walked back through the streets in the middle of the night. Everything he did was for safety, to be sure of survival. But a great icicle that was hanging from a high roof fell and pierced the back of his neck so he died almost there and then. And his death was the greatest gift to Comrade Stalin for it sent out a message of fear to all other dissidents. What if the icicle had not fallen by accident at all? What if it had been planned?

The truth was that there was no totally safe place for me to walk. I had to take my chances for the sake of a child's life. The old order had gone. It had unravelled piece by piece until there was nothing left. There was no more trust. Except that was not quite true. I had trusted Mrs Newman; she had trusted me. Lisa had trusted me; I now had to trust her. The shreds remained. They were precious and they remained—for now. But for how long?

What came to me was there were no cars. I was able to walk in the middle of the street because there wasn't a single one: they were gone. And then it came to me that if there was no power there was no point. How many hundreds of thousands of them had been driven out of the city and then left abandoned, powerless and useless?

All at once I heard a small group of people, still quite a way ahead. I darted into the side of the road and prayed they had not seen me. A path led into a passage between the stone houses, akin to the one beside our own flats, and I hunched there, bent and trembling. I almost breathed less deeply in the hope that it might make me less conspicuous. The strange thing was they did not seem in any kind of hurry. I began to hear their voices more clearly, before they were level with my hiding place. Two men and three women. The men were carrying wooden bats, but the one furthest out in the street was swinging his about him, quite unconcerned. The women were carrying things too, but I could not make out what they were. Metal things that flashed in the light as they passed. I could not work out what they seemed to be arguing about to begin with, but then I realized it was about nothing more serious than where they should go. Almost sounding as unconcerned as though they were out on some Saturday night. Whether they should be heading in to the city centre or not, whether they should turn left or right from here. I felt so relieved I almost laughed aloud. Then all at once they started talking about different ways to kill someone, before their voices were too far away for me to hear any more. Just as unconcerned.

At that moment I remembered my mother. I am not sure why I thought of her there and then; I will never know. But with a stab I remembered her. I was glad she was gone from this world; I would not have wished her to endure so much of a moment of this slow descent into darkness, the loss of everything we had known. I stood tall again as the figures disappeared completely. Then I heard something move behind me and I felt metal against my throat.

"Turn round very slowly or everything's over," a man's voice demanded.

I had little wish to do any different. But as I did turn, I saw that the fellow who held something against my throat (and I was not certain it was even a knife) was a full foot shorter than me and most likely in his seventies. I could feel the trembling of the metal object; it was clear he was more afraid than I was and had little idea what he was doing.

Mercifully he hadn't spoken loudly enough to arouse the attention of the group that had just passed.

I held out my hands and opened them. I looked at him and shook my head.

"I have nothing," I told him. "I promise you I have nothing. I am going in search of a doctor because I am looking after a sick child. Please believe me. If I had something I could give you or share with you, I assure you I would. But I do not."

At once he brought the metal object, whatever it was, away from my throat and turned away, unable to look at me. We were beginning the descent into anarchy, but we had not gone so far we did not remember where we had come from. He was almost embarrassed by what he had tried to do.

Still he would not look at me. He stuffed the object deep in his pocket. All the same, I was not fool enough not to think that this might be some elaborate trick. I knew where the object was hiding and I was watching him.

"What are you in need of?" I asked him. "Tell me what you need especially."

Then he turned back towards me. His great black eyes were sunk deep into his face, circled by rings of sleeplessness. Still he could not face looking at me.

"I need everything," he whispered. "More than anything else, I need hope."

"Then you are hardly alone," I said softly. "Look, if I pass this way again, I will leave something outside your door. But it will not be much."

He looked as though he could not quite believe me.

"Thank you," he said, lost and bewildered, remembering the words.

⊸

I had nowhere to sleep under cover that night. I had no choice but to find somewhere close to the railway line, not far from where I had stared at those drums leaking their poison like grief into the surrounding patch of ground. I moved from there all the same; it was as though I could not quite bear being so close to the horror of that place.

I worked hard to find a softer place to sleep; my body still remembered the hardness of that stone floor in the brick building. And it was a clear and beautiful sky and a windless night. Yet again I thought of Rayne, but with a flicker of happiness rather than anything else. I did not feel afraid, not then. And that was all that mattered. I was thankful for what I had.

I slept almost at once, comfortable enough where I lay on the soft ground. And I seemed to dream almost at once too. I dreamed of my mother, that I was carrying her dead body to the cabin. It was there she was to be buried and I was fulfilling her last wish. And everything was as it had been in my earliest childhood: the lake was alive with birds and I could smell the apples. I went running into the orchard and I pulled down the branches to scent that fruit. I was somehow both a grown-up and a child at one and the same time. And there was no sadness in me that my mother was dead. I had brought her back to this place that she had loved so much; I had done what she wanted. And somehow that was sufficient—having brought her here, having done that, the task was complete. And I was free to wander in that place I loved more than anywhere else on earth, and it was suffused with the scent of apples. Then I woke, broke out of sleep to find myself lying on my back on the bare and empty earth, staring at the stars. And my face was wet with crying.

I left the broken sadness of that old man and I went on to the end of that street. I knew that I had to turn right onto Rowan Road and I did so, my eyes searching everywhere ahead of me. I could not make the same mistake I had made previously: there might well be no second chance. I was learning to live in this new world, and it came with no handbook. I felt the heat of the day beneath my garments; my face was wet with sweat. I was wearing too much. I had brought not a drop of water with me because every drop we still had was precious. But I was thirsty already. There was nothing on Rowan Road except for one single car whose windscreen had been shattered. Somebody had wanted whatever was on the dashboard; something of value. And what was of value now? Almost nothing that had been deemed to be of such worth in that world we had left behind. The great god mammon was worthless, a currency that counted for nothing now. I could have given that old man a couple of crumpled notes and what would he have done with them? Better to have given him a decent weapon, if you really sat down and thought about it. That was the point of insanity that we had reached. I thought of Rayne in the heat of the flat and I hurried despite my better judgement. Now the only thing I had to do was find a doctor; bring a doctor back with me. When I tried to believe in those words they sounded impossible. But at least I had a lead.

I turned up onto Oak Road and bit my lip, willing the street to be empty. I scanned the high windows and saw not a single face. Where were they all now? What had become of a whole city of people? The road led up to the top of a kind of hill; here I was to turn right and follow Ash Road beyond that. The doctor's address was on Sycamore Street: everything was named after trees in this district of the city. I got there; I reached the door. His was a basement flat. And my hands were trembling with fear.

When the man's face showed from behind a door that opened a few inches, I babbled the whole of my story. About a girl and her mother who had come to my flat two nights ago, and how the girl was now sick. Would he please come with me to see her? He did more or less what Mrs Newman had done: he pulled me inside the door and shut it behind me. But before saying a single word he bolted it and chained it. Only then did he turn towards me, his face ashen and his eyes weary. He was perhaps thirty, not more; his fair hair starting to thin. I was standing in a kitchen that was crowded with drying clothes, with boxes, with old shoes. He put a hand on my shoulder.

"Take your time and tell me what you have to. I was asleep and you were lucky to find me here at all. And before you tell me anything else I want to know how you knew I was here. Start with that and then tell me the rest."

I came up for air and breathed. The strange thing was that to my own surprise I found myself close to tears. I told him about Mrs Newman and it was somehow that which broke me; the last thing I had ever have expected. It was the door back into childhood. The door into a place that had been inhabited by my mother and father, that seemed safe and good and true. It felt everything that this new world was not. But I was allowing myself to be a victim of sentiment too, and I knew I had to think straight and speak clearly.

"I am sorry. I did not know the way. Getting here felt a risk. It took a lot."

"Getting anywhere is a risk," he said grimly. "All right, I'm awake now and I don't think you've come here to kill me or get drugs. So sit down and tell me everything from the beginning and I'll do my best to help if I think I can."

We went through to the other room and before we sat down he poured two shots of clear liquid into glasses. It tasted like fire.

"You found your way here," he said. "You made it. Mrs Newman sent you. Now tell me the rest."

❧

He listened. He insisted from the beginning I call him Simon. He smiled when I talked about Mrs Newman, said he had been with her husband when finally he died. And he said he would come with me to see Rayne because of my connection with the Newmans, and because it was not enough simply to hear my ramblings on the subject. That was how he described them and he smiled, told me I could stop being so afraid.

"Preserve that for when things get much worse," he said. "And I prom-ise you, they're going to." Then abruptly he got up, vanished into another room of the basement flat and I heard cupboards banging and feet on stairs.

"Come on then," he said when he returned. "We need to get there as quickly as we can."

We said nothing as we went, and he took us a better route than the one I had used; one that I tried to remember and could not. I still did not feel quite myself; kept going through everything that had happened, both now and years before. The old man, the group I had so nearly encountered, the walk through those eerily quiet streets—never knowing for sure what would happen. More than anything, my knowledge that a child lay sick and getting worse by the hour in my home. And at last, at long last, I gave that knock on the door and Lisa opened at once.

Simon went in and saw Rayne on her own. Lisa stood in the kitchen, turned away, her hands pressed hard on the table. She said nothing and I babbled useless things about everything that had happened that morning. Then there was laughter from the bedroom and Lisa looked round, but not at me. Her face was wet and then suddenly Simon appeared. He closed the kitchen door, sat down on one of the chairs.

"She's going to be fine," he said quietly. "She's got a temperature but it'll pass. I've given her what little I can spare. What she needs is lots of sleep and keep that cut clean. That and a lot of love should do the trick."

⊸

It was strange that Lisa hardly wanted to speak to him. I asked some lame questions, and there was little we could offer him. After a few minutes he scraped back the chair and got up. I rose with him; Lisa stayed where she was.

"Is there anything I can do for you?" I asked. He hesitated before he replied.

"Yes, actually there is. Perhaps you'd have time to come with me. There's something I want you to see."

I glanced at Lisa and she half-looked up, nodded.

"I'll be here with Rayne," she said. "I'll be fine. Thank you for coming, Simon."

Before I went out I remembered I needed water: I was parched. I ran the cold tap and there was a kind of thumping noise before a trickle of water started running. Something else we had taken for granted, I thought. That might be about to vanish too. Simon said nothing more until we had gone outside and the front door was closed.

"I need to talk to you urgently. Is there anywhere we can go out of earshot?"

"Nowhere but the shed in the garden." I laughed foolishly as we stood inside and he pulled the door shut behind us. I could barely breathe for the heat.

"Look, there's something you need to know. Lisa's not just any woman. She's not just some poor victim of a lunatic politician who turned up at your door for charity. Have you not noticed the mark on the back of her hand? Her left hand?"

I had no idea what he was talking about. It was clear he understood that.

"All right," he decided. "I'm going to take you somewhere and it's going to make you understand more clearly. Once we're there we can talk properly. Not for long, and you'll realize why. And after that you're going to have to get back here on your own. So you'll need to remember the way for yourself, all right?"

We went back out into the baking heart of the day and into the open street.

⌁

I think it must have been about two or three this afternoon that the rain began. It seemed to come out of nowhere. For that reason I believed it would not last, that perhaps after half an hour or even less it might be over. I was walking along the railway line, and all of a sudden it came to me that what I was walking towards was beautiful. Had I been a painter, and had I not been destitute at the world's end, I would have wanted to try to capture the symmetry of what I saw.

The railway line ran straight on, heading dead west, or so I reckoned. On either side were the fences, running on and on too until they merged with the thunder grey of the storm clouds. And they themselves were beautiful, at least there was a terrible beauty about them, to use the words of Yeats. It was as though there had been a volcanic eruption somewhere to the west: the whole sky was dark with this vast grey-black mass that at its edges had wisps of grey. And that mass itself was symmetrical. For a minute or so, I stood there doing nothing but looking into that great and magnificent symmetry. And I called to Rayne to come and look, and she ran about ahead of me laughing, telling me I was mad.

And it was as though I woke, shivering, hearing her words in my ear and realizing that she could not have been more right. I was wet and freezing, and I was walking right into the storm. And Rayne was not there. I looked at that moment towards the houses over to the left, and I suddenly wondered why I did not go there and find one. They were all empty; why the hell did I not use one? Nothing in the way of shelter lay ahead of me. The line stretched on emptily into the oblivion of the storm clouds. With numb hands I bent down, picked up my bag, and began shuffling on, towards the hope of shelter.

⌁

There were ten streets to remember before we reached the place Simon wanted to show me. In actual fact there were half a dozen, because up until that point I was still in familiar territory. I learned something else as I walked with him, that not everyone was necessarily going to want to rob a

42

passer-by or attack them. We saw four individuals or four groups of people; they merely kept on their sad way as we hurried onwards. Of course it was much better that there were two of us, but what mattered was Simon's sheer confidence. He knew where he was headed and nothing was either going to stop him or slow him down. I kept the names of the last six streets in my head and I repeated them over and over again. I tried to make some kind of pattern out of them; taking the first letter of each name to create an acronym I would remember, and nothing worked. I gave up on that. What I did know was that I had a good, or at least a reasonable, visual memory. In every street I found one thing to remember, however small. That was the thread I was paying out behind me so I could weave my way back in the end.

Part of the reason, or even most of the reason, I had no idea of the last bit of the city we passed through was because all of it was seriously downtrodden. I would not have walked here with confidence even before the breakdown of our society began. And I knew that my parents would have struggled too. There had been nothing in the least privileged about us. It was as simple as that. Neither my father nor my mother had inherited much in the way of money; we lived simply enough. My father had simply been fortunate enough to inherit a flat in a safe and prosperous part of the city. And for safe and prosperous you could read dull: very little in the way of excitement happened in our district, particularly after nine o'clock at night. Boringly safe was the best way of describing the place where I had grown up.

What I saw about me was now was the sadness of neglect. Those were the words that came to me as Simon and I kept on as fast as we could.

As I hurried through those inter-connecting streets with Simon, trying to find landmarks to remember in each one, I worried about two things: I worried about remembering their names and I worried about Lisa. What had I done by opening my door to her, by effectively letting her right into my life? I realized I had been more than naive. I had not the slightest idea where she came from, in any sense. I had trusted her blindly, with complete faith. Perhaps that was because she came with baggage, namely with a child called Rayne. That changed everything: first and foremost, it altered crucially the way I had viewed Lisa from the moment she first hammered on the door—or perhaps more accurately, from the moment I opened the door and let the two of them in.

When Rayne was asleep, Lisa could go through anything and everything that belonged to me, that had belonged to my parents. She could find out all she wanted or needed to know. It came to me that I was locked out of my own home. Did she need me enough to let me back in? Did she care about me enough to do so? Perhaps the care did not count; the need mattered more. All of it came back to trust, the last shreds of trust in a torn-apart world.

The sweat poured from my face and neck: my head was thudding from the relentless heat of the sun. Now and again I stole a glance at Simon but he looked neither to left nor to right: he kept straight on, swift and not the least anxious. There was nothing in his expression that betrayed a single thought or emotion. I wondered again where on earth he could be taking me, especially in this grim bit of the city. The two of us could not have been more different. In the course of the last two streets I had begun feeling increasingly anxious—anxious about everything. Again, it was all about trust: I had no choice but to trust someone else implicitly. He could, after all, have been leading me to my death.

"This is where we're going." His voice was flat as we started descending a steep flight of stairs. At the bottom he held open a door for me.

⌁

That holding of the door was deliberate. Inside, in this basement that looked like the bottom level of a multi-storey car park, there were hundreds of people. They were crammed together, sitting in the shadows, and their faces turned up towards us as the door opened. It was as though they awaited the making of some speech, as though they felt sure that some pronouncement was going to be made. A silence descended as that door opened and Simon and I descended three stone steps. There was all but no light in the place: the windows had been blocked out. But that made the place cool; there was obviously ventilation or it would have become airless and stifling in no time at all for so many people on such a broiling day of heat.

Simon motioned to a door on the left as I went down the steps. What could I do but obey? In my confused state I opened the door, entered a small room, found my way towards a seat. I looked at him and my face asked the question obviously and easily enough.

"I brought you here so you'd get some sense of what's happened. These are just a few of the ones Gorwel managed to drive from their homes. He didn't do it personally: he got his henchmen and women to do it for him. People like Lisa. And I want to stress this, these are just a few of them. They're homeless: they have nowhere left to go. We've been trying to feed them, and look after their medical needs. The next crisis is going to be over water: you realized that the city supply is on its last legs when you turned that tap on in your kitchen. Give it another twenty-four hours and it'll be gone, or at least what's left won't be safe to drink any longer."

He leaned forwards. "These are ordinary people. The kind you lived beside. They were driven out: for daring to wear crosses, for carrying Bibles. They have done nothing wrong beyond that. Gorwel needed scapegoats and these were the easiest to find. And the easiest are always the weakest."

⊖

"Tell me how Lisa fits in to all this," I asked, looking right at him.

He sighed and glanced away, folded his arms on the desk in front of him.

"This is where I'm on shaky ground, thin ice—call it what you will. I just want to warn you, make you aware of the situation."

"Then tell me how Lisa fits in to all this," I said again. I felt increasingly vulnerable and increasingly confused. I needed to know the truth.

"All right. Gorwel made his speeches at the stadium and whatever he was or wasn't, he was a damn good orator. I said to you that those people out there are just a few of the scapegoats. They're the lucky ones. Many were killed, and in terrible ways. Many fled, simply left. In the first days, at the height of his popularity, Gorwel made converts. Ironic to use that term, but it's short-hand. He called himself The Beast: those who joined up after the speeches were made got what he called the Mark of the Beast. Not because he was paying homage to the Bible but because he was mocking it. An indelible mark on the back of the left hand: a kind of tattoo. That's what Lisa's got.

"Now all those who joined up had to do what they were told. They were given names and addresses across the city. You didn't just join up and go off back home. You had to do your bit. They went straight from the stadium: that was his way of working. Fire them up and send them out. I don't know how many nights like that there would have been. Perhaps ten or a dozen, maybe many more. It doesn't matter. Of course there were plenty who realized what was on the cards and started packing long before they were driven out. That was part of the whole plan, I'm sure. Get them to jump long before they were pushed. It's just that Gorwel didn't bargain for all that was going to happen. But that's what I want you to know. That Lisa must have been involved in one way or another, at some point."

⊕

I had listened to every word and I was thinking, trying to work something out.

"If that is true, then what about Rayne? Lisa is on her own with Rayne, and that child has not been carrying out the orders of Gorwel. So that is the part that makes it hard to believe; I am afraid I would say more or less impossible to believe."

"You're right, and I've no answer to that. I thought about that almost the minute I sat down in your kitchen and saw the back of Lisa's hand. But all I can tell you is it's the mark. And she doesn't even try to hide it."

"And what happened in the end to Gorwel?" I asked. "And to so much of the city? They can't all have fled because they were afraid of a Bible being found in their homes. It has to be more than that. Where have they all gone?"

As I asked the question I remembered what lay hidden in my own home. What if they had come for me? What if that night when Lisa hammered on the door it had instead been Gorwel's mob coming to take me away?

"A lot have gone north, I know that for sure, to try to escape the heat. I can't tell you how many died in the heatwave. And the next one that comes will finish the city, because by then the water'll be long gone. But the fact is that many did flee because of Gorwel. And the irony is that he's disappeared. Not a sound's been heard of him for weeks now. No one has a clue where he is and not a trace of him's been found. And now I have to go back out there and try to look after these people. I told you, you were lucky to find me at the flat. I'd usually be sleeping here with a couple of other medics after working a whole night."

"Thank you for what you did in coming to look at Rayne."

"I hope things work out for you; that you find your answers, manage to stay safe."

46

He got up and shook hands. That was all. I went up the stone steps and out into the baking heat. I felt more confused than ever before in my whole life.

↩

By the time I reached the fence beside the railway I felt utterly drained. It was partly the rain and the sheer misery of the day: it was as though I had been punctured and the energy, the very will to go on, poured out of me. I might have done nothing beyond slumping against that fence and weeping. For there was no hole to climb through as there had been the time before. The fence was most likely seven feet tall and there was no way on earth I could hope to get over it; I knew I would never have had the strength. For a moment I could do no more than hold it with both hands as the rain sang around me; I leant forwards, my eyes closed, drowning with self-pity and despair. And I remembered Rayne and how she had been there and had shown me the hole that was torn in the fence. And as I thought of her now and wondered how she was I asked myself what she would have done. How would she cope with the fence this time? All I knew was that I missed her: I stood there, wretched in the rain, and I just missed her.

But one thing that was for certain was that she would be urging me on; she would be tugging at me and telling me to look, to open my eyes and work it out for myself. And in the semi-darkness as the storm descended, I did open my eyes and stand tall where I had been slumped against the fence. And what I saw ahead of me, perhaps a hundred yards or so away, was a sign, a station sign. I was almost at a station where there would be a path out and no need to climb any fence at all! This was Edgefield, one of the stops in the suburbs, and I started stumbling my way on through the rain to get there as quickly as I could.

It came to me even then in my bewildered state that I could hardly get more wet than I already was. I found my way to the platform and I looked up in sheer gratitude at the white station sign, and hobbled out onto the path that led back up towards the houses where I wanted to go. And I saw Rayne skipping ahead of me singing.

❧

Strange that even then, soaked as I was and chilled to the bone, I hesitated before going into that first house. It had belonged to someone else: it had been a home. So much of our lives is secret; even our closest friends know little or nothing of how we live and love. At least that was the way it was, how it used to be. And that knowledge rushed through me as I stood there, reticent, on the threshold: *This was all how it once had been.* This was not a home anymore; this too was nothing more than a kind of museum.

And it was that realization that finally pushed me forwards. I opened the unlocked front door of an empty house and I went inside.

I began by going through every room. I went slowly and on soft feet, as though carrying a torch in the darkness to look at everything. There were only two sounds; my shivering as I walked and the hammering of the rain on the soft roof tiles. The daylight was starting to diminish now but there was still enough to see by. I do not think I would have remained had I found death there—I still carried the memory of that soul in the brick building by the railway. I had been so desperate I had taken the wood they once gathered and never used. Yet was there any point in feeling guilt over that? Would it have changed a single thing? But there was nothing here. Nothing beyond the photographs of children and the sadness of a kitchen left intact. It was a museum, but I walked it with reverence just the same: it was a place where a family had lived and dreamed. It was as though the memory of many things was imprinted somewhere in the very walls and the floors. In an ante-room there was the stench that came from a freezer, nothing more. And in the bedrooms the beds were even made. At least in the main room they were; in a smaller one a child's duvet lay dumped on the floor and I smiled and thought of Rayne. A laptop was abandoned useless on a table; tablets lay scattered on the floor. But there was not a clue as to why they had gone. All I guessed was that they must have left quickly; that once the decision had been taken that was it.

❧

I began by locking the front door. Then I slowly went upstairs and stripped off all my clothes and hung them to dry along the wooden banister that ran the length of the upper corridor. I took off everything, and spread out each piece of clothing so it would have maximum chance to dry. I could not and

I would not leave the place until that had happened. And then I curled into the main bed, my teeth rattling with the cold. The bliss of lying in a bed again. I brought my knees up to my chest, curled into myself, and blew into the frozen claws of my hands. I thought of the bathroom and the useless shower that stood there, and imagined for a moment standing under an endless flow of hot water.

I realized that I had forgotten to leave the candle holder outside in the hope of gathering fresh water, and I promised myself that I would do that once I had warmed and before I went to sleep. But I could not manage it yet; I simply had to recover some warmth before I did anything more.

Before I did drift into a strange and feverish no man's land somewhere between waking and sleeping, I was aware of the rain's note changing out there on the house roof. It grew almost deafening. I knew there could have been no other course of action but the one I had taken. I had stayed out too long in my folly and I was paying the price for it. At least I had seen sense in the end. What mattered was that I didn't fall ill. The house felt seriously chilled but not in the least damp. The duvet that was pulled tight around me was bone dry. I thought of Rayne again and I saw her suddenly glancing into the room and smiling. I started telling her how glad I was that I had come inside but all at once she darted off again, and told me she would see me at Edgefield. I tried to tell her that I did not understand and she called back that I would. She was impatient and skipped away, even though I asked her to stay and talk. But she only said again that I knew where I would find her, and the only sound left in the silence was the thundering of the rain.

When I reached the door of the flat I paused before I gave the knock that Lisa and I had worked out. I had seen a scattering of souls on that long walk back from the refuge Simon and the others must have set up. Those I did see were hopeless and helpless in those sad streets. But it came to me that perhaps everything that had taken place meant you could not call parts of the city bad or good any longer: such terms were meaningless. Those of us who remained were all the same. One old woman wandered along the road in her dressing gown, shuffling in no more than her bare feet, looking as though she was lost. She turned and looked over towards me with a face that was white and bewildered. And I had nothing for her and there was nothing I could have said or done. No one was coming to rescue her. Neither now nor in the days to come.

All the way back I was remembering what Simon had said. I knew that I was still far too blue-eyed: I believed everything too easily. It was the way I had always been and I was not about to change. But it was an attribute that was of little value now. I was learning and did understand that the wrong move now might well cost your life. And with every day that passed the situation became darker and more dangerous as those who were left became more desperate. And I had trusted Lisa: I had got the measure of her from the word go and I quickly realized that she called a spade a spade. But I had never for a moment considered not trusting her. Yet neither had I thought to ask her any questions, and perhaps in these new days we were living through we all had to start asking questions. I felt I barely knew myself any longer, let alone anyone else.

And so I stood outside the door of what had become my own flat, the place that had belonged to my parents, and I hesitated before I gave the knock she would know. I had gone over my script a hundred times in my head and still I was not happy with it. But I had come home in the end and I had no choice but to give the knock she would know.

"She's asleep," Lisa said, turning on her heel as soon as she had opened the door. I closed it behind me and climbed the stairs, feeling as I did the hard hammer of my heart. When I got to the top she turned and looked at me, folded her arms.

"She's been asleep since the moment you went out the door. I've seen right by your mother; even though I didn't want to leave Rayne on her own I felt I had no choice. The body's lingered long enough. And there's no water left now. I've collected what I could from the tap and we can boil that over the fire for safety's sake. Oh, and then I was tidying and I happened to find something. I found the book you'd hidden there. The Bible."

I opened my mouth to say something and she silenced me at once.

"No, you can listen to me before you say a word. Because I just want you to know that all people of faith are nothing less than enemies to me. And it doesn't matter which lot you think you belong to because one lot's as bad as the next as far as I'm concerned. If you hadn't opened your door to Rayne and me, you know what I would have done to you? I wouldn't have opened it when you came back just now. That's the worst thing I could have done. You'd have been homeless and you'd have died out there, and it would have been one hellish death. That's the only reason I didn't, because you opened a door to us. But I don't properly know who you are and I want you to be damn sure I'm watching you. I'm watching every step you take and I can tell you now that if I have to kill you I wouldn't give it a second thought."

I felt my face draining of colour. I kept my eyes on her; my voice was soft.

"Why, Lisa? Because you have killed before? Because you have killed for Gorwel and his mob? I know all about that mark on the back of your hand now. So we are even. I know every bit as much and more about you."

❦

She held my gaze for a moment and then she looked down, sighed heavily.

"Look, let me go in and check on Rayne and then we can sit and talk. I've drawn the curtains and opened the windows to air the place as much as possible. I need to get her to drink more than anything. Give me a minute."

I went into the kitchen and found a last piece of the cake Mrs Newman had wrapped for us so carefully. It made me think of her life now, of what was left of it, and that felt almost unbearable. We simply had to keep going, that was about all we could do. I found two plates and I cut that last piece of cake.

"We've got no more than half an hour to talk," Lisa said when she came back through. Her voice was low, softer even. "She's less hot; the fever's passing."

"I want you to know I do not feel I know you properly," I said, and I leaned forwards as I spoke the words. "I do not feel I know you at all." The room was dim: the closed curtains shut out the glare of the sun on yet another windless afternoon, the sun that felt like a beating heart, a thudding in the metallic skies. Lisa nodded, looked away.

"I realize that. And that's why I only told you I'd found your book. Yes, it's all right, you can explain later. It doesn't matter now. But the fact is you did let us in, and you asked no questions. We were lucky. It was a gamble that paid off. And I know I owe it to you to tell you more and tell you the truth. It's good timing with Rayne asleep. So this'll be the short version just in case she does waken up and we don't have the chance again for however long, or ever again. I'm not sure how to start, but here goes. I grew up in a house that was completely atheist. Is that how you'd say it? My mother was a really strong feminist and I was brought up tough, learned to look after myself and to look out for myself. My father walked out when I was six, and that made me even tougher. I missed him badly for six months and then I don't believe I gave him another thought. That made me even surer I had to have a thick skin."

-&-

"I mean I didn't decide that at the age of six and a half, but it happened. It was a response. But it's not that I had a brilliant relationship with my mum either. There wasn't a lot of love from anyone growing up. And I recognized the need for love. I looked for it in the wrong places since I found so little of it at home." Lisa stopped a moment, listening. "I thought I heard a noise next door." There was nothing, so she went on.

"Things were beginning to change fast in the world. There was no certainty; you know that too. We had not a clue what was coming next. But the long and short of it is that I left home the minute I could and pretty much broke off contact with my mum and my sister. I felt there were bigger things to worry about than a broken family I couldn't put back together."

She shrugged her shoulders and looked down at the empty plate on the floor.

"Gorwel came at the right time for me. The timing seemed perfect, just as it probably did for a whole lot of others. An angry man who saw where to put the blame for a climate that was out of control, where far too little had been done way, way too late. And after all that hadn't been done by the religious right, we still had these lunatics daring to preach at us! I think I was actually at the first stadium speech Gorwel gave, however long ago that was."

"And did you join right away? Were you converted from the beginning?"

She glanced at the back of her left hand and half-smiled, ruefully.

"I wasn't exactly sober when I got this, and it was bloody sore, I can tell you!"

She shrugged her shoulders again. "Look, what matters is *that* I joined, not *when* it happened. I was young and I was angry. We felt our future had been taken from us and we wanted, we needed, we had to have, someone to blame."

⊷

"All right, but how were you involved? Were you active? Did you do things?"

"I know what you're not asking," she answered, suddenly looking away. "And the answer is yes, I'm coming to all that. I didn't ask any questions at the beginning, leastways not nearly enough. And all the people around me were in the same camp, and that's dangerous. You fire each other up. You get each other going. You stoke the flames."

Again she looked away, down at an empty plate. Then right at me.

"We were sent out in groups, usually five or six of us in each. Sometimes it was a propaganda thing. Graffiti on some mosque or church, and I mean serious stuff. This was really to scare. To make sure they knew we were watching and would be back. Most of it was done in the middle of the night and the police never laid a hand on us. By then they'd been bought anyway. But there were raids too. We broke into places and made as much mess as we could. The idea was always to scare. To make a lot of noise and to leave a place in one hell of a mess: stained glass windows, altars, books. Gorwel wanted books taken out more than anything. If there was one thing he couldn't abide it was holy books. The fact that people could be stupid enough to read some ancient text and believe the world really had been put together in a week. It drove him mad. And then the fact that all those same people who believed in this *wonderful creation* didn't do a blind thing to save it!" She shrugged her shoulders.

I stopped her, lifted a forefinger, sure I had heard something myself this time.

Lisa nodded and got up, was out of the room in an instant. Sure enough, I heard Rayne's muffled crying. And then Lisa's voice, soft and reassuring. So different. That she could change like that, in an instant. Then there was quiet again and I simply sat there, thinking and wondering. She came back in, sat down once more.

"If we're lucky we've ten minutes," she said.

⊷

Lisa gathered herself, took a deep breath, and once more she looked away.

"All right, last bit. The Chinese always say the last mile's the longest mile. It was always worst if we met people. I've said the idea was to scare like hell, but we didn't set out to attack groups. There was no trying to kill folk at services or things like that. But sometimes we did meet people just the same. I was sent on a raid against a preacher and his wife. I don't remember what religion he was and it doesn't much matter. There were four of us. We weren't going to attack them; all we were doing was trashing the house. Nice house, nice area. We smashed our way in and of course we met him downstairs, in the hall. He was attacked, not by me but by two of the others. He was badly injured, left on the hall floor.

"Then the wife came down and begged us not to kill her. She said she had a child, that we had to spare her for the sake of the child. She said a lot. That she forgave us for what we'd done, that she didn't hate us. We could take whatever we wanted. That made two of the group even madder and they just went for her. I won't tell you what they did. They didn't kill her but they might as well have done. And then they ran away. They tried to drag me with them but I wouldn't go. The child was crying upstairs and I couldn't. I remembered what it had been like for me; not having love. The woman was dying; they both were. And I asked her what the name of the child was. She said Rayne, because that's what they'd been praying for; that's what the earth needed. And I said I'd look after her. That I'd take her and be a guardian to her. I'd do my very best for her. I sat on the floor beside her and I promised her. Then I took the child and I went. There was no point sitting waiting there until they came to carry me off. Then the child would've had no one. That was the last thing I did. I had Rayne after that, and Rayne mattered more than books or buildings or any of the rest of it. And then I came here."

She finished and her whole face was angry with tears. She had broken; she had melted. This was what lay inside; this was the part that counted.

I woke up in the early morning and was conscious of my thirst at once. I remembered vaguely that I had forgotten to leave out any container to collect water, and I realized just how foolish that had been given all the rain that had fallen through the night. I drifted back into a dream where I was asking someone in an old house if I might have a drink. I felt cold and afraid as I stood there naked. And it was only a voice that answered me; I was looking towards that voice but I could never see where it came from. The voice answered that I could have a drink if I could prove that I had ever given water to anyone else. That was all I had to do: the only thing. And my mouth was parched and dry and empty. I could think of no one. And I began wandering from room to room in the hope of finding water and there was nothing. And when at last I came to a room in which there was a basin with taps, I turned them in hope and there was nothing. Not so much as one single drop.

So I lay there in the dark of the early morning, somewhere between two worlds. But I was warm; I had slept for all of ten hours or even longer, and I lay wrapped in warmth. And little by little light began filtering into the room, and what I saw ahead of me on the wall was the blown-up picture of someone smiling. One of the children who had lived in this house once upon a time perhaps, or a cousin or a friend. That smile in the strangeness of the morning. And then as I lay there staring I knew that I had to find something to drink. I got up in the rawness of the early morning and found my way carefully downstairs like a blind man. I fumbled in my bag for the candle holder and I unlocked the door. After a moment my bleary eyes realized that there wasn't so much as a single cloud in the sky after that long night of rain. And my dry mouth twisted into smiling at the sheer strangeness of that.

Lisa went to see to Rayne and I sat on where I was, thinking about everything I had heard, trying to make sense of it. What mattered more than anything was that she had told me the truth. But I was not sure if it made what happened now easier or harder. Perhaps that wasn't even the question: the next step would simply be what it had to be. I was grateful for the silence, the space. It was as if the last days had not held so much as a moment to stop and draw breath, to think. My life until then had been almost the complete opposite; even once the world began to change and the old certainties began ebbing away. I had been aware of the outside world, but not part of it. Somehow it remained far away. Now there was no outside and inside, or to put it another way, the outside had poured in and it would have been impossible to shut it out again. I felt as though I had aged by several years in the course of the last months, but I realized I would hardly be alone in feeling that. It was just that my life before had been so strange and isolated I was struggling to cope with having been thrown without warning into the real world.

I listened to the softness of the two voices in the room next door and the strangest thought came to me. I wished it might have been possible to paint them. To capture the gentleness and tenderness of the voices of a kind of mother and what might have been her child in a painting. Even more so because now I knew the real story of that child. And I thought of a Rembrandt and realized that it had been done, as much as such a thing was ever possible. Yet not so much that you could actually hear the muffled loveliness of the voices of a mother and her child through a wall. It had been done and it would most likely never be done again.

All at once Lisa was back and it was as though the outside world had rushed in once more. But she didn't sit down: she came over to where I had been sitting and it was me that stood up. And her voice was soft.

"I've made up my mind. I'm going out and I'm leaving you here with Rayne. I've no choice but to trust you. I have to separate all my prejudice from the evidence. And I've not a shred of reason to doubt you. But the fact is one or other of us has to go out there and find food, find water. Whatever the hell we can find to get through the next days. And the difference is I know where I can go. One place for certain, and maybe somewhere else. The difference is I've got to know people in the city over the last however long. Some of them may be dead and others may have gone. But I know the places to look for them."

"But I would have thought you would be an outcast to them?" I said. "After everything that happened in the end. After what you did."

She nodded. "I am to most of them, that's true enough. But there were one or two who understood, I know. They saw things had gone way too far. They may have kept their mouths shut for the sake of their own skins, but they knew all right. The question is more whether they're still here or not. But that's why we have to go and find out and stop wasting any more time. The water's run out and that's going to make one hell of a difference."

I nodded. "And how is Rayne? Is she stronger? How is she doing now?"

Lisa smiled. "She was singing to herself. She has a pretty stone she always carries in her pocket. Light blue. I think it's sea glass. She was holding it up above her face in bed and turning it round and round, singing away to herself. But the poor mite's thirsty. That's when it dawned on me just how much we need to find water, and fast. And then move. This place simply isn't safe enough. We need to find somewhere else, somewhere higher up."

↢

The door at the bottom of the stairs closed. I listened to the silence before going in to find Rayne. I had asked Lisa what happened if she did not come back at all and she just looked at me. There was no answer to that question. We did not know the answer and we could not think about the question.

"I am glad you are feeling better," I said when I had sat down with Rayne. "We were worried about you. I am glad I was able to find Simon to look after you."

Rayne did not seem interested in that any more. It was all over.

"Did you always live in this house?" she asked instead, and I nodded.

"What do you think of it?" I asked. She looked all around her, rather critically.

"I think it's a sad house. I think it needs more laughing." She looked still at the walls and ceiling, like some professional who measures a house's happiness.

"Well, I think you might be right," I agreed. "But it was not always a sad house, you know. When I was your age and lived here with my mum and dad, there was lots of laughter." I thought about what I had said and was not sure how true it was. Perhaps it was more what I wanted to believe was true. It certainly had never been a particularly angry house, but it certainly had been quiet a lot of the time. I remembered the safety that quiet had given me. A kind of gentle web. It had all been about the inside and the outside. But not any more.

Rayne was still looking at the walls and the ceiling as if she could tell pretty much exactly what sort of house it was from the paint that had been used.

"It really was not a sad house," I told her, though I am not sure she believed me, or even that I really believed myself. But all at once I thought of something else.

"Come with me," I said. "I want to show you the place where I used to play."

And I took her up to the see the attic under the roof. It was too hot and stuffy to stay there for any length of time, but she was intrigued all the same.

"Did you play here with lots of friends?" she asked me, and I shook my head.

"I played inside my head, Rayne," I told her. She looked at me for a moment, thinking about what that meant, and then she nodded.

⟿

I wanted to do everything I could to make her forget about her own thirst, and about the fact that Lisa had gone. I dare not even think what I would do, what would happen, if she did not come back. But I had to push that fear out of my mind. We could not think like that. We had to believe, and go on believing.

All at once I thought of something else and went to an old cupboard in her room. It was low to the ground and I got down on hands and knees to open it.

"You know what I'm finding for you, Rayne—it is the bear I was given when I was a baby. And I loved this bear so much one of its eyes fell off."

Rayne hooted with laughter at the thought of that. She was holding her stone to the light again, and her face was all screwed up. Then she turned round.

"I had a bear once," she said, as though suddenly remembering. She was on my level as I sat there rummaging in the drawer. She had forgotten all about the blue stone now. Her voice sounded somehow strange and far away.

"And what happened to it, Rayne?" I asked, and as soon as the words were out I realized how stupid they were. But it was too late. Her eyes welled with tears and it was as though she broke into pieces. I held her in my arms as I knelt there on the floor, and I cursed my stupidity for not thinking about the whole home, the whole world she must have lost such a short time ago.

"Where's Lisa?" she asked through a mask of tears, her voice utterly forlorn.

"She will be back as soon as she can be, Rayne," I promised her. "She has gone to find us things we need. But I will be here and I will look after you, I promise."

She nodded and rubbed at her eyes. "I'm just so thirsty," she said.

I nodded. "I understand, I know. Let me find the bear, and you know what, then it can be yours. I want you to look after it for me from now on."

✦

I remembered Rayne's thirst as I crouched outside the house where I had stayed that strange night. My mouth was caked with dryness and there was a terrible sourness to it. But I crouched there still just the same as the sun began to rise in the eastern sky. This was what used to be called winter. The snow and the frost were gone and forgotten; they had been washed away, and all that remained was the dull ache of cold, a rawness that would not diminish and that seeped into the marrow, deep and sore. But that was why I had chosen to leave when I did. It would have been nothing less than sheer madness to start walking under the summer sun of this new world with no knowledge of where fresh, safe water was to be found. It would certainly have been suicide. This alternative was bleak, but it was bearable. All the same, it did nothing to take away my thirst right now.

I felt like an animal going round the house as I did in that next half hour. I crept round it, searching and hoping for water that might have fallen and gathered somewhere, water that would be safe enough to drink. And as I went, the sun rose in the east. To begin with, it was masked by thin trails of cloudlike smoke. That made it possible to look full on the ball of the sun as it climbed, beautiful, into the white-blue of the sky.

I crouched there for a time, for all the world like one of my own primeval ancestors, watching the majesty of that ball of orange glowing as it rose and went on rising. Then, thirst made me carry on the pitiful search for water, and before I had gone the whole way round the house I had found an old plastic pot that had half-toppled over and was edged with dirt and green growth. But it was brimful of water just the same, and I knew it must be rainwater from the night before. I closed my eyes and drank greedily what would have been a cup full of water. And as I did so I remembered Rayne.

✦

I found the bear that I had promised to Rayne and I babbled away about it, hoping all the time I might be able to take her mind off her thirst just a little. It was a frail hope, but I had to do my best all the same. I found that bear at the bottom of a cupboard full of games and old clothes, and things that had been put there most likely because there was no space for them anywhere else. That was one forlorn bear. Not only had one of its eyes gone, but the tummy had been ripped so the stuffing was coming out. Yet for a moment Rayne did forget; she pulled the bear out of my hands and leapt back into bed with it.

She was already feeling sorry for it and talking to it, telling it that things would get better in the end. And I crouched there on the floor for a moment listening to her, wondering if those were the kind of things Lisa had said to her that day. I listened to that sing-song voice of hers talking to the bear as I stuffed all the old things back into that bottom drawer. In truth I was just grateful I had kept the bear at all, for it had obviously fallen out of favour early on, probably after it had begun falling to pieces. When I was done I pushed the drawer back in and I turned round to Rayne. Then all of a sudden I remembered something.

"There's a bit of water next door but I need to boil it first, Rayne. I'm going to make a fire first and once it is ready you can have it to drink. All right?"

Her eyes shone as she turned to look at me. "Can't I just have it now? I'm so thirsty. Please can I have it?" Her whole face imploring me.

I bent down close to her. "You do not want to be sick again, Rayne, and nor do we. It has to be boiled first so it is safe. We do not want to have to go and find Simon again to make you well, do we?" I ruffled her hair. "The sooner I make the fire and boil the water the sooner you can drink it. All right? Now you stay here with your bear and I will go next door and get it ready as fast as I can, I promise."

She looked at me with big and anxious eyes, that ruin of a teddy bear held in the crook of her left arm. She said nothing, just looked at me, and I thought in that moment what must be passing through her head. All she had grown up with had been ripped away from her and what she had been left with was a place where every day was different. She had known me for all of two or three days, and she had no choice but to learn to trust me. All I could do was make sure that her trust was never betrayed. I smiled to her and what rushed through my mind were imagined images of the kind of childhood she must have known. The safety of a house where there was nothing but love. A house of faith where grace was said before every meal. A house where voices were never raised and things were not said in anger. Then all of it ripped away in the course of a single day; the start of a new life where nothing was certain any more. Except that Lisa was doing everything to keep the promise she'd made.

"Shall I say a prayer with you, Rayne?" I whispered, and she watched me all the time and did not blink. She nodded and kept on watching me. I took her small hand in mine and I bent my head and closed my eyes.

"Dear God, we ask you to keep Lisa safe and to bring her back soon. I ask you to be close to Rayne and to bless her. I ask that she may be really well now and I thank you for her. Keep all of us safe and in your care. Amen."

I heard her breathing *Amen* too, and when I looked at her she was still watching me with those huge brown eyes. I smiled and ruffled her hair. She did not smile but just kept watching me. If only Lisa would come back soon.

"I will go now and make the fire, Rayne, and I will be as quick as I possibly can."

"Will it take five minutes?" she asked, turning as I stood up to go.

"It will take the same time as it takes a teddy bear to wash and dry his hands."

She hooted with laughter. Then she looked at me and nodded, and I thought what trust was still there that had not been destroyed.

After I drank I stayed there, crouched close to the ground, eyes shut, just breathing gratitude. I set that pathetically dirty plastic vessel upright where it might gather new rain in the night. I would not be so foolish again. I walked round the last part of the house and by now the sun had risen above the thin mist of cloud low in the eastern sky. Already that sun was too bright to look at directly. I stood there, eyes closed, drenched in pure golden light.

In the end I went back inside and locked the front door without thinking. The living room smelled sour and sickly because of whatever things had rotted in a freezer that no longer worked. But I forced myself to stay there all the same, even though I hardly knew why. I was searching for something. The laptop was dead and there was no point wasting time with that. So were the tablets that had been left behind.

But I was suddenly aware I had only scanned the place in the semi-darkness of the previous evening, and now I could see in proper daylight. I found it hard to look at the portrait of the family on the wall. They would smile there for eternity: that frozen moment of happiness. It meant nothing now; it was no longer real. Or did it remain real in some strange way? As long as I was here, as I stood watching it? As long as the picture lived?

Then all at once I saw the torn shred of paper lying in the corner of the chair.

> *I know this message may be pointless, may never be found. So I'm not sure why I'm leaving it, unless someone comes here looking for us. We are going north. We are taking the car and will drive as far as we can. The problem is going to be charging the car again and what we do when that's no longer possible. It's over forty degrees now and we cannot stay here any longer. We are too afraid. I cannot say why we are so afraid: that is all I can write. We are being driven out. All we can hope and pray is that talk of R318 may be true. We are taking everything that we need with us and we will not come back. There is nothing left to come back for.*

I worked on the fire with trembling hands. We had paper in plenty and for the moment we had matches; what we were desperately short of was wood. In the end I scoured the flat for something, for anything, that could be sacrificed. Even then I could not find it in me to take one of the more precious antiques and start chopping it for firewood. My mother and father were too recently departed. The time would come when I could do it, and probably it would be soon enough, but I did not feel I had got to that point yet.

What I did find was an old wooden box that had been special to my mother in her childhood; something for keeping trinkets—treasures that had been given to her or things she had found. It had been scratched and knocked about: now it felt the equivalent of that bear of mine from the bottom drawer. I had the box broken and reduced to splinters in seconds: it was thin wood and tinder dry. My hands were shaking by the time I lit the first match: I had set the fire so I knew it would take at once. My hands were shaking because I wanted that little girl to have the water she so badly needed. I had promised her.

But the fire did not take, or at least it did and then something was damp perhaps and the flame turned blue-green, then diminished and went out. I swore under my breath, crouched there like some caveman, and my hand shook even more when I struck the second match. The flame crept and grew.

I could hear Rayne's voice through the wall as she sang and talked to her bear. The bear spoke back to her and though I listened, I could not catch the name she had found for it. Then my fire crackled and spat at last: I willed the pan to begin bubbling and at last it did. By then Rayne's voice had long since gone quiet and once I went in there at last with a big cup of cooled water, she was lying stretched out on the bed, her teddy on its face beyond her outstretched left hand. And I could see in the half-light of the room that her face was stained with crying. I woke her gently and finally was able to help her to drink. As I spoke to her softly the knock came at last on the door downstairs.

↢∙↣

"Water, candles, matches, disinfectant, cloths, food." Lisa put everything down on the work surface in the kitchen in triumph. Rayne had been beside herself to see her: they had spent the first ten minutes laughing and tickling each other, the bag Lisa had brought home left splayed and forgotten on the kitchen table. Lisa had to meet the bear first; learn its name and a whole lot more.

"People are leaving," she told me. "All of them seem to be heading north, or so it looked to me." She thought about her directions and settled on that.

"They're not going to get far, that's the worst of it. They can't carry much in the way of water; nothing like enough to last them. Once they get out onto the open road, it doesn't really bear thinking about. It's only a matter of time."

"And where did you find all this?" I asked. I was still euphoric that I had been able to make the fire and boil that water for Rayne. I wanted other things to count, but it still felt that this was what mattered most. I was still trembling.

"I went to two places. I'd stayed in both of them before I had Rayne. The first one was all smashed up; I don't know what happened. Looked as though it's been derelict for days now. I didn't want to hang around there long: I felt it was better to get away. The second place belonged to Jan and Pete. They were part of my group but they sort of understood what I did. They gave me all this. It's not a lot, but when you think they didn't have to give me anything at all . . . . They say there's still talk of R318 and rockets, that they'll go. But we need to find somewhere better, safer. We're just too

63

vulnerable here. Somewhere away from the centre, and a hell of a lot higher off the ground. That's what matters more than anything. And the thing we have to get is water."

"I will go tonight," I said. "And I will try and find somewhere. I have a place in mind."

She looked at me and nodded. I had almost hoped that she wouldn't.

⟳

"I had wanted to try to tell you about the book," I started. She frowned.

"I don't need to know about it now. Somehow it just doesn't feel it matters. All that's been left behind. I still believe Gorwel was right in what he said. I'm less sure about what was done. But I'll go on believing just the same that the lion's share of all this (and she jerked her thumb towards the curtain and the world behind it) is the fault of the religious right. The mess we're left with."

But she caught herself again and frowned. "It just doesn't matter. Now it's about nothing more than surviving, about finding enough water for a child and for ourselves." She put down the cup she was holding and looked at me and her voice was soft. "We've gone beyond all that. What matters is that I can trust you and I know that I can. Let's leave it at that. I'm not judging you, nor you me."

I nodded. I wanted to tell her all the same what the book and the words meant to me, but somehow I did not know where to begin. I was not sure she would understand. She was right that we could trust one another and right too that this counted more than anything. Perhaps my words were best left unspoken.

"Tell me about R318," I asked instead. "I know something, but not enough."

"Oh, it's some planet they've discovered and think could be inhabited. A planet where we could start again. I have no idea how long they've known about it, had their eye on it; who knew what when. I talked to Jan and Pete a bit; we'd maybe ten minutes at the most, not much more than that. No one knows anything for certain and there's still not a word of Gorwel. Everything started falling apart fast, that's the thing for sure in this whole wretched mess. It's like dominoes: once the first one falls everything else follows." She shrugged her shoulders. "Jan and Pete want to go, if it's possible. I'm not sure what choice I have. Not with things as bad as they are now. I need to be there for Rayne."

She said she was going to look in and check on her and I thought about what she had said. I felt there were no choices now. Only roads that opened up if we were lucky. Then it was nothing more than a case of hoping the road we chose was right.

✧

The evening came at last and I decided to do something when Rayne and Lisa were talking in the other room. Their voices somehow like fur: gentle and comforting in the middle of all that was lost, all that we did not know. I found candles and I lit them. Then I broke up more pieces of wood and I made up the fire again. The heat was going out of the day at last. I looked behind the curtain and the sky was strange, like infected skin. There was a yellowness to it; a wrongness. A yellow-grey wool of silence. And below it the slow moving of small figures. Matchsticks leaving to move north, against the hugeness of that terrible sky. I could not look and yet I could not look away. Until I closed my eyes at last and let the curtain fall back and I re-entered everything that remained here, all that we had shored up against an almost certain end.

I went and found Lisa and Rayne, and I was told the bear was now called Simon. And I smiled and said something to Rayne while in my mind's eye I saw again that great basement room and its refugees and thought of Simon, the doctor. I blinked the memory away and I told Lisa and Rayne I wanted them to come with me next door. I heated water in one of my mother's ancient pans over the fire, and I made Rayne a steaming cup of hot chocolate. She held it in her small hands and she looked into the dancing of the fire. The bear had to have a little of her hot chocolate too, and she chattered about everything and nothing and we sat there, the three of us, in that shadowed room, and were all right. Those were the two words that came to me: *all right*.

For it could not hope to last, not for long. But what mattered, some-how all that mattered, was that it lasted for now. Because we cannot and we must not remain prisoners of time always. We must be able to slip free into places that are out of time and beyond time. And I do not know how long it lasted, and that does not matter. All I do know is that I never wanted it to end.

When I had read the message that family had left behind in the house (and not once but many times) I put it back exactly where I'd found it. This was their last will and testament. All I wished was that I might have known their names. They would always remain nameless. I looked again at the portrait of them on the wall, their hands touching as they smiled and looked out with such happiness at an invisible photographer.

I asked myself what I was going to do now. I could stay here one more night before I began walking again, but only one more, because I must keep moving or I risked being trapped. I would lose the sheer courage to keep walking and I would end up dying in some no man's land like this. I simply could not stop too long. And when I did start walking once more I had to decide if I was going to keep following the railway line or if I would finally strike out into the woods. I had come to the edge of the city now; it certainly could not be long before I found the courage to leave the safety of the line and face the woods. I had no idea what I would find there: that was the real reason for my fear.

There was one thing I should do now, before making any decisions. I should find fresh clothes. The ones I wore now were filthy. The family who had lived here would have little use again for what they had left behind. They had known they were never coming back. I told myself that and yet I found it difficult even then. All I could do in the end was to open drawers and cupboards with a kind of reverence. I opened them not as someone who assumes or who takes for granted. I found fresh things that were better by far than what I had left with the day I walked from our refuge on the seventeenth floor. And I took an extra sweater for the nights that lay ahead: the unknown nights. And before I left those rooms I breathed my thanks to them, these nameless ones.

I went in to say good night to Rayne, who was lying in a warm bed, clutching her one-eyed bear. I sat down beside her, smiling, and stroked the head of that battered old bear I had never thought I would see again. I remembered something.

"You know the story of Noah and the Ark?" I asked her. Of course she did.

"Well, in a way I think what we are doing now is a little like that."

She thought about what I had said and frowned. "But we don't have a boat."

"No, you are right, we do not have a boat. But I still believe it is a bit like the story of Noah and the Ark just the same. We made a mess of everything, so the weather changed, and now we have to try to do everything we can to save what we have left. I wish you could see the cabin where I used to go when I was your age. It was a little house made of nothing but wood. I had my own bedroom, much smaller than this one, and there was a window at the foot of my bed. And at night I had a candle in a lantern. It felt so exciting going to bed. From my window I could see the lake. That was the most special thing of all. There were geese and swans on the water all the time, and if I was really quiet when I went to the river that flowed into the lake I would see a kingfisher—this beautiful bird that was blue and green and red. They are all gone now; there are none left. So that is what I think, Rayne; that we have to be a bit like Noah and find all those good things and keep them safe. I think we have to do that more than anything else."

And as I told her all that I believed it too, but I had no idea how we would achieve it. I was not sure it was not too late already.

I suddenly realized that Lisa was standing in the doorway listening. And I remembered that I had been talking about a story from the book. But she had not tried to stop me all the same. It was too late for worrying about that, just as she had said. And Rayne was fast asleep.

⊷

We heard the thunder long before I had left the flat. Somehow I had known what lay in that yellow sky, somehow I just had not realized what it might mean.

"Go safely," Lisa said, and for a moment I thought she might hug me. Her eyes glittered and she looked at me a second before turning away once more.

I did not tell her I was going first to the house of the old man to whom I had made the promise when I went to find the house of the Newmans, even though I knew next to nothing about him. I was aware my promise had been foolish beyond words, but I faced the stark reality of the fact that I was expendable. Much as I cared for that child, Rayne needed Lisa far more than she ever needed me. I was not intending not coming back, but if for some reason I didn't . . . .

I could hardly believe how hot it was. That airlessness, and the far muttering of the thunder. If there was to be a real storm, it might break the fetters of that heat for a few days. I looked up at the city clock and saw it had stopped at six minutes to eight—now in reality it was more like midnight. I heard the sound of someone weeping and did not even think to stop, but I was conscious of the fact I had not done so. I was changing; all of us were, just at different speeds.

I thought of that man with the knife I had passed in the doorway and willed him not to be there. I found the place where he had been crouched and saw only a stain of blood on the stone. It was another story to which I would never know the ending. Then I remembered my own rule to keep to the middle of the street until I came to the place where I had gone into the side to avoid the gang of five youths. I found the old man's door and left the bag outside. I hesitated and then knocked a single time before fleeing. There was pitifully little inside that bag. But I had promised. Perhaps he was already dead in a city that had run out of love and run out of water. The sky flickered with lightning as I went back to the street.

Where was I to go now? Lisa had offered no suggestions about the seeking out of some new refuge. The only thing I did know was that wherever it was it had to be much higher above the ground. It had crossed my mind to think of another flat in the building where I had grown up, but I knew Lisa sensed we were also too close to the centre of the city and felt uneasy there. For my part, I wanted to find somewhere in a place I knew; I almost did not quite know why. A knowledge of familiarity? From nowhere came the memory of the one real childhood friend I had had growing up, a boy called Douglas. He and his mother had lived in a block of flats that I visited now and then, not often. I loved taking the lift to the twelfth floor where they lived. It was the one thing he hated because the lift was forever break-ing down. Ashwell Court.

I went back to our street first and slipped into the shed where I had stood last in the heat with Simon. I had to stop and close my eyes and remember exactly where Ashwell Court had been. I had to visualize the walk to get there. One link in the chain I could not remember for certain, and that was because it had always been the point when Douglas had had us jumping a wall to take a short cut. But I reckoned it could not be more than twenty minutes away, and a safe enough location. If any of that mattered now, and most likely it did not.

I never met a soul. I saw one body in the street but I did not have the courage, or the folly, to find out more. The thunder muttered in the skies; I was pouring with sweat from the exertion of climbing one pathetically small hill and yearning for nothing more than a full bottle of ice-cold water. I came to the towers: five of them standing like sentinels over the city. And not a single light from one of them.

I knew in the dark which Ashwell Court was and I crossed the wind-still grass to approach the entrance. And as I opened the glass door on the ground floor a figure rose up in front of me and held what I could see and feel was a real blade against my throat. All I could do was hold up my empty hands.

"Give me everything you have right now," she said, for it was a girl that spoke.

⌁

"I have nothing," I told her, stressing each word as I spoke and meeting her gaze as I backed off, the knife against my Adam's apple. Even then I was aware of the trembling of her hand. A moment later and that hand had dropped, though the knife was still pointed at me, glittering in the dark.

"All right, I don't care what you have or don't have, you're coming with me. Into the building. No, don't speak, or I'll use the knife. That's right, and up the stairs first, facing me so I can see you. Keep going, keep climbing. We're going to the thirteenth floor so it's a long way. Don't look anywhere else but here."

Kidnapping was a good deal worse than other things I had imagined happening. I was ready in some kind of a way for violent encounters, and I suppose I knew that if such an encounter was serious enough then it would simply be the end. I still was not really aware what lay beyond the walls of the safe place where I had grown up. Or perhaps in all conscience I had not truly grown up at all.

We passed a body in one of the stairwells, a body that had begun to smell already. I went on climbing, backwards and upwards until it hurt my calves and I had to raise one hand and beg that we stop. I breathed a long torrent of words about why I needed time: she gave no sign of doubting me and waited. I guessed a great deal about her on that backwards climb to the thirteenth floor.

I had to stop a good many times on the way, and on each occasion I observed her as we stood on our respective stairs. I watched her a great deal more than she watched me. At one point I wondered if I should topple down, taking her unawares, and hope to knock her over as I escaped. But I lacked the courage and I could see the knife had a serious blade. If that were to spear me on the descent it would be a long and bloody crawl back to the flat. Fortune favours the brave. I reached the thirteenth floor still debating whether to try or not.

᠅

"All right," she said, steadily and softly, as we stood together at last in the half-dark of the landing. "I'm Anna and my brother's Michael. He's seriously ill with something and I don't know what it is. All I need you to do is be here so I can go and find food and water. I can't leave him on his own. We're going inside."

I stopped her, poured out a torrent about how I had come in search of a place, somewhere for a child that had been ill too. They would be out of their minds with worry if I did not come back, if I disappeared. *Please, in the name of God.* My appeal fell on utterly deaf ears and the heavy black door was opened and the knife pointed at me in the darkness. I realized this might be the last chance in a long time and I thought yet again of hurling myself into the stairwell and hoping to escape. But what if I fell? Then I found myself inside.

The place smelled really bad, so much so that I felt dizzy with sickness. A single pathetic candle flame fluttered on a low table in the centre of the small room. All at once I remembered the flat where Douglas had lived. This was little different. A hand reached out to me across the table; a slow white hand.

"Hello, my name's Michael. I'm sorry Anna had to bring you in like that, but there was no other way. I'm not good and she couldn't leave me here alone."

I could see his face now. Eyes huge and set deep in the white fear of a face. Either he was trying to smile or else what I was seeing was his pain. I had sat down but Anna remained on her feet. I still felt like retching.

"He's got a child and the mother; he was looking for somewhere to stay. I've told him why we need him. I'll wait till dawn until I go out and start searching."

He was just watching me, sitting hunched and afraid like some injured creature. This pathetic look on his face; this gaze that held me horrified.

"I beg you to let me go," I said softly, forcing myself to keep looking at him. "I simply have to go."

⊕

"We'll let you go as soon as we can, it's as simple as that." It was Michael who spoke the words, not Anna. She was still standing, watching him all the time.

I felt desperate. "Look, there are refugees everywhere. The city is falling apart and it isn't safe; not going out alone. If you let me, I would get things for you—and I promise I would do. But I have to go back to a child and her mother. Please."

I tried to look at both of them in turn, but she kept watching Michael and he would only look at her. "Please," I said again, bent towards them over the table.

"Let him go, Anna," he breathed and my heart leapt. I leaned forward, all ready to say more and offer more. But Anna crouched down in front of him.

"No," she said fiercely. "We've waited for this chance, this moment, for three long days. I won't go back on that, Michael. I owe it to you to look after you and you know that's what I'll do. We've been through all of this. I will go out at dawn and I will come back—and will *only* come back—when I've found all that we need. Look at me, Michael. Look at me and tell me you understand."

Suddenly it flashed across my mind. "I know a doctor!" I told them. "He came to see Rayne, my child. I could try to find him, bring him here. Please!"

Michael was looking at me again and suddenly I realized just how ill he was. There was something wrong, something that did not work, behind those eyes. They were not just looking at me, they were stuck and glazed. She was pulling him away, turning him round and trying to get him to lie flat. Talking to him all the time and stroking him, as a lover would. I could do nothing but watch.

And outside the thunder padded about like some caged beast, wanting to break free at last. I was so thirsty and I breathed through my mouth with the stench of sickness that was in the room. What the hell was I going to do?

"We'll talk once he's asleep," she breathed to me, turning as she did. And as he lay there, I caught sight of the mark on the back of his left hand.

I went downstairs in the fresh clothes, knowing that once I was outside and walking again I would most likely feel I was wearing too much. But I had spent so long being cold and raw, it was good to feel warm again. As I came downstairs, I heard the tapping fingers of rain on a skylight window. That was helping to make up my mind about the coming night. I could not face sleeping in the open that night.

I sat down again in the living room and was far away in my thoughts about that letter the family had left behind, as the rain drove over the city in clouds.

I jumped, certain I had heard a voice. "Hello?" My mouth still dry and useless with thirst. I staggered out to the front door, looking. Nothing. Broad daylight and the same silence. I locked the door again to make sure and came inside, but I did not sit where I had before. I went upstairs, to the room where I had slept the night before, as though there was greater safety in that. Was that how I had left the duvet? I sat and listened, holding my breath and listening.

I was thinking about *them* all the time, wondering what had happened to *them. There will be no coming back from this.* I heard the voice in my head and the litany of the words. Where were they? Where were they now? I did not want to think about them and yet I could not help it. It was as though there was no choice; as though their own words they had left on the paper had brought them back. It was as if I could catch their shadows and sense their presence in the rooms that had been theirs. I had to move. I had to do something. I could not sit here and lose my nerve. I had managed however many nights under the stars; I could surely cope with a couple of days in a house. I went out the back door, almost beside myself, into what once had been a garden, and I did nothing more than walk, despite the last spitting of the rain and the sheer bleakness of the day. I looked at the back windows and the mess of weeds that choked what once had been a flower bed. Something was growing there, a vegetable I recognized.

෴

I had no water with which to wash them once I had ripped them out of the ground with trembling hands. I was still racking my brains for their name, but it had gone and it didn't matter. They were edible, that was what *did* matter, though heaven only knew what toxins must be in the ground they had grown from. They had gone to seed, that much I knew. I recognized them from their green; it was a kind of shining on the leaves, almost a luminescence.

I brought them inside, my two hands cupped together to carry them all. Because I had no water I stripped off far more than was necessary. It did not matter; this was still a feast after days of hunger. And I felt that hunger rising within me; I felt the wetness of my mouth. I found some other old piece of clothing and scrubbed my hands on it madly. I ate like a wild animal. I saw myself as I stood there bent over the sink, unable even to have the patience to go and sit down. I stuffed my mouth with a crunching of something green and rich. I ate every last fragment and felt good. I was sure I felt stronger.

That night I went to bed early. I had found a bottle of brandy at the back of one of the cupboards and had allowed myself two small glasses, but it was way too much just the same. It dizzied my head and made everything that was in my head flow together. I missed Rayne so much that the missing streamed in two rivers down my cheeks. She was not there and I missed her—no one was left now. Everyone I had loved had been taken away, was gone. I was so alone.

I went to bed and in the night I woke and sat bolt upright, sure I had heard a voice. I held my breath and listened to the silence, as the frail rags of the wind flurried about the house. But there was nothing. I lay down once more, almost wishing that someone had been there nonetheless. The dark had become too vast. I went back to sleep after a long time: I felt lost and strange. And I wandered through whole roomfuls of dreams, looking always for the same thing that I could never find again.

~

Michael was asleep and Anna let go her hold of him, let him slip like a doll from her arms. He was skin and bone. It had taken little time for him to drift away. She came over all the same and sat beside me at the table, still whispering even though it was needless. The knife was nowhere to be seen.

"Gorwel is dead," she told me. "They found his body and there's no doubt he was killed. He had his enemies in the end and they'll find them. They'll go after all those who went against him. They will root out every last one of them."

I heard my heart as I spoke. "But how will they find them? The place is falling to bits. People are simply getting out. It's the only thing that matters now."

She shook her head. "That's not what Michael says, and he should know. Yes, there's chaos. But they'll go after the ones who're still left in the city."

And I thought of all that Lisa had said about having to be higher up, about getting away from the ground floor. I thought of Rayne asleep where she was and I could hardly bear it. If only I had chosen a different one of the towers. I would have been back by now and we could have left even then, escaped the wrath of whatever beasts might be ruthlessly rooting out Gorwel's enemies.

And for the moment there was nothing in the world I could do, nothing at all. And I was next to useless here on this thirteenth floor keeping watch on a dying man. I forced myself to think and talk, to keep my head clear.

"What are you looking for? What is it that you need so badly?"

"Michael wants to end his own life. He has no wish to go on any more. And he also knows it would be better to kill himself than risk dying at the hands of the worst of Gorwel's thugs. I'm going to find the things he needs."

"So he went against Gorwel too?" I said. A statement rather than a question.

She nodded. "He knew he'd gone too far. He had to find a way out."

❧

I was not tired and Anna said she usually sat up for most of the night keeping watch on Michael. All I yearned for was coffee: the thought of it, the memory of it, entered my head and was hard to banish again. Anna had crumbled fragments of biscuits, nothing more. They had come from a neighbour who simply knew more people in the city, having both relatives and friends here.

"Michael and I came in from the country," she told me. "Lured by the voice of Gorwel. It was an act of rebellion too, though. We'd grown up Catholic, but our parents were never strict. We had relatives who were tyrants: we just wanted away from it all. We were excited by everything Gorwel was saying."

I nodded and thought of Lisa. And I realized too that Anna and Michael must have carried out actions too, and done what they were told. He had the mark on the back of his left hand but she did not. I was about to tell her about Lisa, almost certain they would have known her, would remember her. Then it came to me just how foolish that would be, considering the circumstances under which Lisa had left. She must have had far more enemies than friends after what she did. I realized I knew nothing whatsoever about the circumstances under which she had finally got out. I realized she would have had to escape with Rayne.

Michael slept on. He murmured sometimes in his sleep and his wrists and face flickered, and I wondered through what kind of corridor of dreams he wandered. We sat together, Anna and I, watching him and saying not a word.

"You can sleep a bit once I'm gone," she said. "He'll be out till ten perhaps, it's impossible to know exactly. He's been three weeks like this, in terrible pain."

The skies to the east were turning bloody and grey. She got to her feet.

"There's a little water in the kettle that's safe to drink. And there's the biscuits. You can go as soon as I come back." Then the key turned in the lock.

❧

I heard Anna's steps on the stairs and remembered how I had arrived in this place only a few hours before. Then she was gone and there was no sound left. I sat, looking out of the window at the orange-red traces of fire in the east, somehow beyond tiredness and in another place. I thought of a verse from the book I loved; one I had learned by heart. I used to whisper the words in the dark of my room as I lay there. For their own sake, for no more than their beauty.

"And he shall be as the light of the morning, when the sun riseth, even a morning without clouds; as the tender grass springing out of the earth by clear shining after rain."

And I thought, as I had done so many times before, how I wished I could go back to a time when things were still beautiful and undamaged. When the water was not diseased and muddy with toxins; when the air was not leaden; when there were clouds of butterflies and skeins of geese came crying back on the very day they were supposed to return. And whose fault had it been? Who had broken the chain, the chain that kept every part of it in place? It was *all* of us; the mark was there on the left hand of each one of us. It did not belong to a particular group or some certain sect. That was nothing more than making scapegoats; the easy solution. This blame was shared: it was as simple as that.

I drifted into shallow sleep there where I sat on the sofa as those first spines of the sunlight came the colour of honey across the city. I was in a boat and rowing with a single paddle; I could hear the splash of the water every time I pulled the paddle back. And I was rowing towards an island, an island where I knew it was all right. Those were the words I heard in my dream. Everything was broken and destroyed and useless behind me, but on the island everything was all right. Yet long before I'd even caught sight of the island I came to, and when I did waken I was staring straight into Michael's strange and broken eyes.

"What will it be like?" Michael asked, and each word was like a crumb of dry bread. I did not need to ask him what he meant because I understood at once. I knew that he meant death and all that lay beyond; I was certain of that.

"I sat with my father when he was dying," I told him. I knelt on the floor in front of Michael, and took his thin hand in my own; five fingers of bone. I took that hand with the black mark on it, whose meaning meant nothing any more but which must have caused so much fear and hatred and suffering. I thought of Rayne: it had taken away nothing less than her whole world.

"My father had believed in nothing," I whispered. "But he believed in beauty. That was why he went out and found the book for me, the Bible. Not because he believed the words but because he loved them. And he made the cabin with his own hands, the place where we went every summer. Where the singing swans had come, and the ice. He had believed in beauty and he had made it. He had carved it out of wood. And when he lay dying he asked me to read to him and I did, from the story of creation. And he said nothing at all when I had finished, but I saw something all the same. I never told anyone; didn't even mention it to my mother. But when I finished reading and closed the book and looked at him, I saw the light in his face. The room was dim, it was almost dark. But all I know is that a light came into his face when he died."

Michael's eyes looked at me, and for a moment that look was real; it was not glazed and lost, sunk beyond pain. And I knew that he had heard me.

It was only a moment later the key rattled in the locked door, and it opened and Anna came in. She carried a syringe, and she had a small bag in her other hand.

She looked at him with huge eyes.

"You can go now," she said.

The moment she released me I ran. It was still early, barely morning, for Anna had taken far less time than I had feared she might. But before I was gone, before I had started down the flights of stairs I had climbed so painfully the night before, she told me something. And I realized as I turned to look at her, and as I saw that wreck of a man lying there yearning for death; as I looked at both of them in the half-light of the morning against the window, that they had changed in the space of those few hours. They had begun as people I knew at the end of a knife and by the end I had begun to love them.

"The seventeenth floor," she said. "The flat on the seventeenth floor has been empty for a whole year. You could find that as a safe house for the child."

I nodded and I thanked Anna. I would go back and find her, because I knew I would not see Michael again. I prayed she might still be there; that Gorwel's spies didn't find the place too late and take out their wrath against her.

I realized Gorwel's ring of power must have been a whole lot tighter than I had imagined. It came to me as I ran that I had no idea who Lisa had been with just before she came and hammered on my door. I realized now she might well have been escaping. I had not thought of how she first came to the door, nor had I thought to ask. I had not seen a need to know. But now I just ran; I pelted through the silent streets, not caring any more if it was foolish to run. I had to get there in time and we had to leave that place before it was too late. All I saw was the same hunched body in the street; all I heard was someone else's crying. But I did not stop or so much as slow down. I just kept running until I was there.

"Where the bloody hell do you think you have been?" Lisa blazed at me when I had knocked and prayed the door would open. I poured inside to her and the child, and Rayne hugged me. She was smiling from ear to ear, and I barely heard the questions that came in a whole torrent. Because they were all right.

We had to think what we needed as fast as we could; there would be no coming back. I was high on adrenaline: I must have slept for all of one hour the previous night, yet I felt alert and aware and present almost as never before. Rayne danced about Lisa and me suggesting things. It was all an adventure. One thing that was certain was that her bear Simon had to come with her. I bent down to her level and said that Simon could come as long as he carried the piano. Rayne hooted with laughter and told me she would talk to him, and proceeded to do so. Lisa and I started packing together in the kitchen. I wanted to tell her what I had heard from Anna but I could not find the words. Perhaps what mattered was that we were going, that we were moving to a new place and were a step ahead of any who might know where she and the child were.

I forced myself to think of what we needed. Everything precious had to be forgotten and everything practical remembered. Lisa and I would take rucksacks: I had found them in another ancient drawer in Rayne's room, but they were old and strong and would hold plenty. They would be sufficient.

"What was that?" Lisa said all of a sudden as she was lifting a container, and Rayne stopped dancing with her bear as though she had frozen in mid-air. And her eyes welled with tears because she was suddenly afraid, because doubtless it brought back too many memories. Lisa dropped the utensil on the floor and went to her and held her until the two, the woman and the child, melded and became one. I went downstairs and I listened and I held my breath and I heard nothing at all. It was as though she was hearing all that I was imagining.

"It must have been the wind," I said lightly, looking up at Lisa but saying the words as much to Rayne. We went on and in as little as half an hour we were ready and on our way. And the last thing I put in my rucksack, right at the very back, was the book. I went and found it myself and did not say a word. That was the one precious thing that came with us. Then we had left, like three shadows; began weaving our way through the streets towards the tower blocks.

⊷

"This will be my room," Rayne decided. She and the bear bounced on the bed.

It was clean and it was quiet and it was safe. And it was almost at the top of the tower block; I think there must have been twenty floors altogether. It had felt strange passing the thirteenth, thinking of the night before and of how I had left them in the end. Strange to think too that had I not spent that night with them I would never have known of this place of safety higher up.

We could see a long way from up here. I took a long time getting used to being so high up; did not so much as like looking out, though I said nothing aloud. We could see as far as the railway line—and that was a long way. I remember standing there at the little side window, wondering just how long it had been since a train had run there. Rayne came and found me and looked too, and she told me that foxes liked railway lines. I looked at her and asked her how she knew that and she just shrugged her shoulders as though everyone should know. Then she was off again; she could not keep still and could not stop exploring, and all of it had to be done with her bear. Then she went and found Lisa and told her she was very, very thirsty. Lisa came in to where I was standing at the window and we looked at each other.

79

"I'll go and try and find Jan and Pete," she said softly. "If I draw a blank I'll keep searching, come back as soon as I can."

Just then Rayne entered the room. "Will you two be all right on your own?" Lisa said, bending down to take her up in her arms.

"We will be just fine," I told her. "We will have an adventure up here on the seventeenth floor and we will look forward to you coming back to find us."

I knew exhaustion was going to catch up with me in the end; I knew it would have to. But I still felt wide awake now—alert, alive. So much so it was almost like an electricity, a static I could sense the whole time. And I had a day with Rayne, this little girl who felt now almost like the child I had never had.

⟁

I locked the door once Lisa had gone. There was silence in the stairwell.

"What will we do today?" Rayne asked, swinging her legs as she sat on the living room table. The rope of her red-gold hair bounced about behind her. I had asked myself the very same question, but her sitting there gave me an idea.

"We are going to build something, you and I," I told her, and I thought again of what my father had built, and how he had wanted to tell me at the very end of his life, how it had mattered so much to him. He had loved beautiful words and beautiful things. And I knew I really had grown up with two useless hands.

But I could build a story.

I cast my eye over the furniture we had. A table, a few old chairs, cushions. We needed more. I opened the few cupboards there were and found boxes, the kind of kindling perfect for starting a fire. They would do. In another I found ancient sheets that smelled dank and heavy after being shut away too long, but they would do just the same. I brought them all out into the middle of the room and Rayne got the idea in the blink of an eye.

"Can Simon help with the building?" she asked. She looked at me intently.

"I'm not so sure," I said frowning. "I did ask him to bring the piano from the old house and he never did. I think perhaps he is a little lazy, so if he *is* going to help then he really does have to promise to do quite a lot of work."

Rayne was not going to answer for him and she rushed off to her room to find him. They were deep in conversation when they came back.

"He says the piano was too heavy," she told me, but when I looked as though that might not be a sufficiently good excuse she added: "He promises to work as hard as he can now." She looked up at me to see how I would respond.

"Well, that is good," I said. "The three of us will work together, and I am going to take you on a journey to my cabin, the place where I went every single summer on holiday. Because I want you to know exactly what it was like."

⌁

It was the table that had first given me the idea. It was simple enough: long and quite narrow, with four strong legs. That meant there was plenty of room for Rayne to crawl about underneath. It was already a house. I fitted a small carpet inside, made of folded sheets. Then I set about making a window that Rayne could look through. That had to be made from one of the boxes, and I took my time carefully carving out a frame and tearing away the bottom of the box. Then I stood it up at one end of the table, the end facing out to the real window from the seventeenth floor. I was just beginning to get accustomed to being this high above the world. Finally I brought Rayne the pillow from her room and got her to lie in an imaginary bed under the table with her bear, looking out through the pretend window to the real one. She added her own refinements: there had to be curtains on the little window and these were more difficult to make. But we got there in the end after I found two old cloths under the sink in the kitchen. Then she was content enough with the result.

I crouched down on the floor beside her, beyond the room the table made.

"So this is what it was like, Rayne. I used to waken up really early in the morning and I would be able to hear the birds down on the lake. I got dressed so nobody heard me and I walked incredibly quietly because I did not want to frighten the birds or the animals. In the summer the sun was shining on the water so it was silvery-gold. And there was not another sound in the whole world. Just the birds singing in the trees. I can remember that from when I was four years old."

"I'd like to go there," she murmured, as she gazed out of the little window.

"This is the closest we can get," I breathed, "by going in our imaginations."

⟿

I wrote all this down in bed after the second night in the house. It was a chance to catch up with my story before I was outside once more and into places where it was uncomfortable to sit to write or the rain made it next to impossible. Even after that strange second night in the house when I had felt so eerily aware of the people who had once been there, I did not want to leave in the end. Not once the day returned and my childish fears had been banished. Hard to close a door on safety and comfort and the loveliness of a real bed and exchange all of it for the cheerlessness of nights in the open and every unknown danger of the dark. But I got up in the end. I had to make a promise to myself that after I had caught up with my story, once that was done, I would set off once more. I went back into the garden before I left and searched for more of the strange vegetable whose name I could not remember. Only one or two pathetic fragments of leaves remained, but I brought them inside and ate them every bit as greedily as I had the others. The day hung still and grey; it was what my mother used to call a nothing day. I wrapped the extra sweater around the book and I took a deep breath to thank the house for what I had found there. I knew I was leaving the city now. I had no knowledge of what I would find beyond. That was the shadow I felt over me more than anything.

Was it for that reason I found myself turning back to the railway station at Edgefield? Was my excuse that Rayne had said she would find me there? Whatever the reason, I left the path and went down onto the platform: there was no sign of her. Then in a single bounce she had leapt from the bushes at the side to give me the biggest fright she could. And I caught her, held her. But she told me at once we had to go back along the path and into the woods. And I had known that all along. It was just that I had been too afraid to do it.

☙

"Jan and Pete are going north," Lisa said. Her voice was low there where we stood together in the kitchen. Rayne and her bear were miles away under the table, though it might not have been a cabin any longer. All I could hear was her voice scolding the bear. I tried to concentrate on what Lisa was telling me.

"They say there are going to be rockets to R318, that things will be much better there. What do I mean? That there's water, food, hope—I suppose a place where there might be some prospect of a future. How do they know? I suppose because they're still in touch with what remains of the group. And you were right; there have been killings after Gorwel's death. Anyway, they gave me an address and that's the place where we've to get to, if we want to go north too. I can't decide for you, but I have to take the chance for her sake."

She tilted her head in the direction of a singing Rayne without mentioning her name in case she might hear. I nodded and understood. I only wished it might have been possible to take them to the cabin and to have that as a home together for a time—or for the future. But there could be no future there, and I knew that. It would have been madness to think so. That was why I had told Rayne all about it rather than Lisa. Because it had to remain make-believe.

"So are you coming with us? Will you travel north too? I asked if there'd be a place for you, and they said yes. But you'll have to make up your mind."

I nodded and looked away. I did not know; I was not sure. I had to think. I went back through to the living room and squatted down to play with Rayne, to enter her world. It was a running away, an escaping from my own head. And perhaps it was a kind of saying goodbye. We were all learning to say goodbye so easily now. I became a bear with a deep voice and Rayne hooted with laughter. That was the irony of it all. A world that had changed forever had brought me such beautiful and precious things.

☙

I lay in the darkness that night and did not want to sleep. Lisa stayed with Rayne in the smaller bedroom she had chosen. I was afraid of sleeping even though I had gone beyond exhaustion and there was something in my head that kept pounding.

And then all the broken pieces melted into one another in a strange land: I was holding Michael's left hand as the syringe entered his arm and he spoke to me as he slid away. Now I was going with Simon into the basement chamber but instead we kept descending into the earth itself. And Simon turned and told me that it was because of the Mark of the Beast. Yet in the end, the tunnel began climbing once more and all at once I found we had broken out there on the seventeenth floor and Rayne was curled up under the table with her bear. She told me that this was the cabin and this was where we had to be. Except that her voice became my father's and I could clearly hear the words he spoke: *"I made it with my own hands. I made the wood for it myself and nobody helped me. I wanted it to be for always. You have to go there. This place is finished. You need to take the book with you. This place isn't safe. You have to go back in the end and I want you to take me with you."*

Then slowly I realized I was listening to the soft murmur of Lisa's voice: I recognized it and could not understand why I was hearing it. Until I wandered out of that strange landscape of dreams and understood that she was there, that her voice was real. She was holding around me and I was crying even though I did not know why. She had gentled her voice and her warmth held me and I closed my eyes because I wanted to keep every moment safe and precious. I slept, as in some shallow sea, that rose and fell with her breathing, with my own. And in the end, hours and hours later, we hailed the coast of morning as it never was before.

I had no idea where I was. For the first time I felt truly lost. As always Rayne had danced ahead and disappeared; I had long since left Edgefield station behind now. There was a soft rain falling. I stopped in the end to do nothing but listen to it, as much because I was out of breath as anything else. I felt old before my time: I had less and less strength in me because I was eating so little. I stopped and stood there, my chest heaving until it calmed at last. I forced myself to stand tall and look around me. The rain pattered and sang in the leaves; a song in the stillness. For there was no wind and there were no birds. That is what came to me at once: there were no birds; there were none left.

All at once I realized these were not ordinary trees but rhododen-drons, at least for the most part. Great lengths of branches with their waxy leaves. They looped into the shadows so it was hard to see where one ended and another began. It suddenly came to me why they were here at all. Once upon a time there had been great estates on the edge of the city, estates that must long ago have fallen silent, their grand old houses crumbled and their driveways grown over; old ghosts from a time lost and long forgotten. And in front of me now there was no path whatsoever. It was just a no man's land of small hills completely covered in rhododendron. And the rain's song softened the silence. I did not know where to go and I was afraid of walking in circles. I still had a sense of my direction just the same; I was aware that Edgefield lay behind me, more or less, and that I was heading south, which was what I wanted.

There seemed no alternative but to wander on in as straight a line as I could manage until I had broken out on some proper path. Because I was sure it would only be a matter of time before I did. Not all of them would be forgotten, buried, and lost. It was just the time it took, and the energy it drained.

It was only perhaps about half hour later that I found myself on the avenue; not the kind of path I had imagined or even wanted to find, but it was something. I had battled through so many bushes I was exhausted; I had breathed a litany of stupid, empty words and hated my own frailty for doing so. Then, without any warning, I broke out of that tangled mass of branches and leaves that I had been pushing from my face and arms for what felt like an eternity. I stepped out and onto an avenue that ran perfectly straight to left and to right of me. And despite the long silence of the new world I had grown to know, I at once involuntarily looked to each side before I stepped out into it. Then I turned to look to the left and the ancient house rose up with its grey turrets and broken roofs, its empty windows like eyes that had been blinded. That was suddenly how I saw the whole house, like the wreck of a man, the great sadness of his face leaning forwards, his eyes gouged out. There should have been crows that scrawled across the sky above the building but there were none. There should have been the shrieking of jays as they flew in their strange undulations, their blue-edged wings flickering. But there were none.

The house was another extinction, something else that had died out. This was its skeleton; left here in the woods until time had taken its bones too, brought them back to the earth out of which its bones had first been made. And I did not have the courage to go any closer. It was as though still I might be trespassing. That was the thought that came to me. For all that, I could not move either. I stood there in the avenue, looking and looking at what once had been and was now no more. And I did not want to go inside. I was too afraid of the ghosts that I would find there—not real but imagined. What came to me was that now it was too late. There would have been a time to go inside but now it was just too late.

Even after that it was not easy finding a path. The avenue was of little use to me; it ran straight from east to west, and would have petered out soon enough anyway had I tried to follow the arm of it that led away from the great house. I did not go inside the place, but in the end I did see that it would make every sense trying to seek out some kind of track that might run from the south side of the building. As I got close to the walls I found I could not so much as look up. It was that childish fear there might be a figure at the empty window; not even a real ghost but something from deep in my own imagination. It was not only this place: everywhere had become haunted by the memory of what had been there before. My idea had been sensible enough. There was indeed some semblance of a track winding through the entanglement of bushes and trees to the south side of the house.

It was a track and not a road; something created perhaps by generations of children's feet, or by the shoes of servants who had walked in to work at the big house. It was a bit better than nothing, but not a great deal. It was becoming overgrown and showed just how long had passed since last it was used. I was heading roughly in the right direction now, but I wanted better than that. I was all too aware that my strength was not going to last forever. My days were destined to get ever shorter.

And then at last I came to a sign that I could not read. I tried to stroke away what I thought was mud from the small metal arm that pointed in the direction I wanted to take, and I found it was not mud at all but rust. I tried to think what name the letters that were left formed and I could not think. I stood there, looking and looking, unable to work it out. Then I realized I was missing the point. What mattered was not the name but the fact that this was a real path taking me in the direction I wanted to follow. And beside the path was a pool of fresh-looking water like a spring. I went over and crouched down and drank.

～

Rayne was thirsty; we were all thirsty. The child was still half-asleep; she wanted to stay in bed and Lisa did not make her get up. When might such a chance come again? They sat together in the room that Rayne had chosen the moment she came into the flat, and the duvet was packed tightly around her so her face was the only thing that could be seen. I said I would go and look for supplies, but that was not the only thing I wanted to do.

"Be careful," Lisa said softly, and her hand just brushed my own. I nodded.

"I'll give the same knock we have always used when I am back," I told her. It was as much a chance to think as anything else, to work out my own mind. How could I make any decision with Rayne chattering beside me in her sing-song voice to the bear? I had to be alone with myself for a little time at least.

Lisa came out with me to the door. "We've to be at the address Jan and Pete gave me at four o'clock at the very latest. That's when the group will leave."

I could work out the question her face was asking but I only nodded again. Then I closed the door behind me. I was not going far for now; only to the thirteenth floor. I heard nothing but the sound of my steps as I descended. I took my courage in my hands and knocked, held my breath as I listened. There was movement inside and perhaps as much as two minutes went by. Then I knew that someone was standing behind that door. I knew without any doubt. The question came: the voice pale and wary. I said softly who it was that was there. Anna opened the door and let me in, closed it again at once. I saw immediately that there was no Michael. She whispered to me to sit down. She did not look at me and her face was wet with grief.

"They came to take him away," she breathed, answering the question I had not wanted to pose. She was looking at the place where once he had been.

I nodded, had thought as much. Then I dared to ask what I had long wondered.

"Anna, was it Michael that killed Gorwel?" She looked at me now and nodded.

"That's why he took his own life," she said, looking at me now. "He was no coward, but he was afraid of what they'd do to him all the same, and he was afraid of what that would do to me. And he knew he was dying as it was. There was no point playing the hero. Better for him to end things than for them."

It was something she had said that night when I was with them that had put the thought into my head, that had made me think it must have been him. *They've found his body and it's certain he was killed.* I had remembered them.

"And what will you do now?" I asked, and looked at her. For a long time it was as though she had not heard me at all. Her two hands lay white and unfolded, turned upwards, and she stared at them without blinking. And then it was as though the words reached her at last; it might almost have been that she was somewhere underwater and sound was different there, slow and strange. She looked at me and it was as if her eyes were no more than empty caves.

"I don't know," she said, answering as though the question had never occurred to her until that moment. "I've nothing left to live for."

I did not know what to say and so I told her about Rayne and Lisa. I told her about the hope of the rocket, that they would go north. And then I had no more to say and I fell silent and she looked away once more.

"R318," she said at last. "What a beautiful name. The best science could do; a letter and three empty numbers. After everything that we had here."

Then I remembered the thirst of a little girl; I remembered I was thirsty too.

"Can I bring you anything, Anna?" I asked her. And she shook her head, as though even that was an effort. I did not know what else to say, and I swam away as far as the door, my head dizzy, as though under that water too where sound was not the same. Yet at the door I hesitated as my hand reached out to grasp the handle. This would be the last I saw of her, or perhaps anyone else. I turned and went back and knelt down and held her hand in my own.

"Goodbye," I whispered.

I went down those flights of stairs without much sense of what to do next or where to go. It was fine and good wanting peace and time to think, but I knew that with every day that passed the city was becoming more danger-ous. There might be fewer people but they were more desperate. We were drifting further and further from the security of everything we had taken for granted.

I tried to think of others we had known in the old days: I flicked through the pictures of their faces in my mind. In truth we almost had not needed such closeness: my mother and father had been best friend to the other. It had been that way from the beginning and our few rooms, a single floor above the world, had been a small haven of safety and quiet talk and silence. Of course there were people we passed and greeted in the street; the taxi drivers and the shopkeepers and the librarians, but none of them was close, someone to whom we could entrust our life. I reached the bottom of the stairs and had no answer, and my mouth had grown sour with thirst. I had to find water for Rayne first and foremost, and I had to have peace to think.

I thought of going back to look for Simon but I lacked the courage. And I also knew that he was caring for a basement full of displaced people, if they were still there. He would not thank me for turning up to ask for help again. Perhaps what I did not want to face was that it had become a time for theft. The seeking out of friends and neighbours; that time had passed. Now we were rats creeping in the corridors for the fragments that would allow us to survive. There could be no niceness any more. There had to be subterfuge and deceit and theft.

I stood at the bottom door, thinking that it was just here Anna had held the knife to my throat. Already it seemed such a long time ago. A few days in this new world seemed so much longer: I felt I had known Lisa and Rayne for years. And then I realized what I would have to do.

I found myself going back to the flat, the place where I had grown up. I went to find something, anything that was precious. Not precious in the old sense, because all that had gone now. Trinkets made of gold and silver, en-crusted with diamonds—such things were worthless now. Nor was selling as it had been since the beginning of time: dirty notes and coins were of no use any more. Yet perhaps it *was* going back to the very beginning, to a time when what was valuable had a different meaning, could purchase food or water or matches or fuel. I imagined now the value of one whole dry box of matches. It was priceless, something that might be fought to the death for.

As soon as I came through the unlocked door on the ground floor I knew they had been there. I had not been thinking about that at all; I had almost forgotten my fear of Gorwel's retribution and the danger to Lisa and Rayne. We had found safety elsewhere in time, that was what mattered. But the moment I was inside I remembered, and I knew. Not one shred of evidence, but I was certain all the same. I climbed the stairs without a sound, and not because I believed they might still be there. I hardly breathed as I reached the hall and opened the door to the main room. And I saw it at once: the table had been scored deeply with a knife. The Mark of the Beast, black and sure.

I took with me just three things: an axe, a pair of shoes, and a blanket, and I fled with them. I put them into another ancient, worn-out rucksack and I banged the bottom door behind me. All I knew was they were what were of greatest value in that place of useless antique books and mirrors. And they had not been taken by Gorwel's mob. They had come for one thing, and when they failed to find what they were seeking they had turned in fury and gone.

The axe was of worth as a weapon and would cut wood. The shoes were good and new: unworn. The blanket would comfort a future without electricity, of raw nights. At that moment the first sun came pouring from the east—low and fierce and blinding. Even now the heat that burned in it was building. I ran despite all the voices in my head that told me otherwise. I had a long way to go.

I went not to a best friend but to a worst enemy. I had not thought of him for long enough, because when school days were finished at last I put my gym kit and tie at the back of the deepest cupboard, a bag of memories I never wanted to disturb again. Of course, I could not know if he would still be there in the house to which I had gone for several years. Once upon a time I had wished him dead, and now I had to accept defeat and go crawling back. All I knew was I must break every promise I had made to myself.

He had done horrible things, for I knew that in truth he detested children. He did not really want to teach them but to make them suffer. He liked fear for it made him feel bigger than he was. He lived in that lonely upper storey feeding on his own darkness.

What had not changed was the scent. It was like opening a small and long forgotten bottle. The scent of the stairwell; the scent of the very dark.

I crept up the stairs and felt twelve years old once more. I had never told my parents what he did: my father wanted me to learn and he found the money to afford those lessons. But I knew well they cost him too much, and I had been afraid of letting him down. Every week I had come down those stairs, promising myself this was the last time, that now I had to go home and tell. And the next week I would return, my heart in my chest like the flapping of a caged bird. So why was I going now? Why did I even think this was a solution? Did I know that if I found him there he would give me what I sought, even if I had to offer more than I was bringing? All I know is I found myself there, at the top of that flight of stairs, my hand preparing to knock as always. And I heard the playing of the piano as though nothing had changed, and the same voice telling me to come in.

He was thin; thinner even than I remembered him. His mouth sagged and I smelt his breath in the dimness of the room. And it came to me that it had always been dim there and had always smelled the same. His eyes were dark and empty and deep-set in his face. On top of the piano by the metronome were the pink spectacles he had always worn. Once upon a time I had imagined them as the spectacles that might be worn by some sadist of a dictator. And he did nothing more than just keep looking at me.

"So the dog crawls back to its vomit," he said, and his eyes never left me.

And I looked again at the metronome and I remembered time. I thought how precious it was and how little I had. I brought the bag from my shoulders and like a strange Raskolnikov I showed him the axe, the shoes, and the blanket. But he did not so much as look at them: he just kept on staring at me and I saw something else in his eyes, something I had tried so hard to forget.

"Why are you bringing me these?" he said, in a tone that a teacher keeps for a pupil; a melding of many things: disdain and boredom and impatience.

I had wanted to tell him about a child, one that was thirsty. And now I knew it was the last thing I should ever tell him, my enemy. I did not want him to know about Rayne: I did not want so much as her name to be tainted by him. I said only I wanted water, as much water as he was able to give me.

"I'm not doing some deal with you for these," he said, as though I must be a bloody fool for ever thinking he would. And still he looked only at me.

"But I might give you water if you let me touch you." And I stood there and I cried as I had not cried for all the times I had been there before. I opened myself and I cried for this last time. And when he went and found what I had asked for he smiled, and it was a smile of the purest triumph.

And I hid in the basement, shivering like a dog. I hid in the shadows that stank of urine and rats. I crouched and I felt just twelve years old, and I was sick over and over again. There was nothing in my stomach and it was as though I vomited up the filth of all those years and was empty at last. I felt weak and dizzy but something had left me just the same. I had faced a fear I would never have to face again, and I had let go of the past. It was as though all of it, everything it meant, had been washed away at last.

In that moment I knew clear and bright what must be done. It was to say goodbye. That was the one important thing that remained and had to happen before it was too late. I picked myself up from that filthy place; I staggered out and upwards and back into the light. For the morning was made of gold and I felt new, released from an ancient captivity. I did not have to hurt any longer.

I ran back and I have no idea how I had the strength still to run. I had barely eaten or drunk for days, and I had passed a point of all proper awareness of hunger or thirst. But I ran with a small bottle of water in my hand for the sake of the life of a small child. I did not matter anymore; I had found my healing but I myself did not matter. I had gone beyond the small and empty things of a world grown weary of itself. I had burned through into somewhere beyond that felt beautiful. Yet it did not lie outside, in a broken and battered earth. It lay inside, somewhere I had not truly known before. And for that I kept running. But when I had climbed to the seventeenth floor, unable to run any longer, and bent forwards as I heaved to breathe, I found that they were gone.

⬦

So I turned and descended those flights as recklessly as I dared, the water bottle clutched in my left hand. And I thought of Anna as I passed the thirteenth floor; I wondered what would become of her after the death of Michael. But I did not pause to listen at the door; I could not. I thundered on down the stairs, the address that Lisa had given me the only thing in my head.

I ran on empty. There was nothing left except the knowledge that I had to say goodbye. I had no idea what the real time was; the city clock had frozen for eternity at six minutes to eight and that was all I knew. I saw nothing; my eyes were everywhere at once as I kept running on through the middle of the streets. I was ready for knives now; even though I did not carry one myself I knew enough about desperate people since I had encountered them and because in truth I had become one of them myself. But what I noticed more than anything now was the smell, the smell of a dying city. And the thin trail of acrid smoke that rose from somewhere, eerie and silent. My chest felt on fire; I heaved for breath as I got there, as I battered my fists against a door and half-collapsed against it. And I heard voices far away as I was dragged inside and faces swam in front of me and I was aware of the banging and the bolting of a door.

Lisa held me and her voice was gentle, there was no blame. "I wanted to say goodbye." And somehow I knew those were my words, that I had spoken them.

Then the face of Rayne, down at my height as I rose onto my knees. She was holding her one-eyed bear and her eyes were dancing. This child who had seen too much; she was still alive and remembered how to love and laugh.

"Rayne, I brought this for you," I said, and managed to smile. "I wanted you to know I am going to the cabin. Remember we made it together? Well, I am going there and I want you to think of me because I will be thinking of you. I want you to be there in your imagination. And I want you to know I will not forget you."

And I closed my eyes and I hugged that little girl with her rope of red-gold hair, and she hugged me. But when I opened my eyes again, and they were half-blurred, I saw she was chattering to a man in that busy house of people, and I guessed it must be Pete. A girl came up and was laughing with her too, and running her hand down that long rope of hair, and I was sure it would be Jan. And I cried now with relief, because I knew it was going to be all right. I thought of the expression *to be in good hands.* And I saw their hands, as they held her and guided her and cared for her, and I knew without doubt they were good hands. In a new world where somehow good had to be born again.

Then I remember speaking and being on my feet, yet hardly knowing the words I did speak. It was as though those words were given to me and I spoke them. Then a door closed and I remember nothing more than lying down on a stone floor and the pain it gave me in the left side of my chest. But I did not care and I slept and time had no proper meaning any more. When I woke up I lay there for a long time doing no more than breathing the stillness, and when I sat up at last I found some food and water beside me, and a key. The key shone bright and silver in the dimness of the room, and I could not think what it was for. But beside it was something else. A red flower that was made of paper. It had five petals and was flimsy, made of tissue. And the red had been coloured in by a child's hand; you could see that at once for the edges weren't exact. And I reached out with a trembling hand to hold it, for I knew whose gift it was.

I sat on that stone floor and ate and drank and breathed until I had the strength to get up, and even then the room swayed dangerously. Then I took the key and the flower as though in slow motion. I went back like a shadow to those rooms on the seventeenth floor, and suddenly I had all the time in the world. I walked as though in slow motion, and I encountered not a single soul.

How many days did I stay there? For how long did I put off leaving? Nights and days no longer had meaning, they slid into one another. I kept what strength I still possessed by sleeping; often I must have been gone for twelve hours or more at a time. I would waken and listen to the silence and drift back into a world that beckoned me, an underworld of old shadows. I saw the faces of those I had known; I recognized them. They looked at me; white and strange they watched me from their no man's land. And though not a word was spoken they told me in the end I must go back and begin. Nothing was said aloud and yet I knew those were their words. One morning I lay there and wanted to slip away and was sure that if I did it would be the end. This was my last chance and I had told Rayne; I had made her a promise and she had nodded. She had understood and would come with me; something of her would be with me.

I did not go back to sleep. I sat there instead in the main room; I sat beside the very place where Rayne had hidden, in the cabin we had built together from a table and an old box and with the help of a bear. I sat there and looked out into the grey nothingness of the morning and then I moved. I got up and went over to the side window and looked down on the edge of the railway line. And I thought I caught sight of the face of a fox, though I will never know if it was real or imagined. I crouched there a long time and then I made up my mind. *I had nothing left to lose.* They were the most liberating words I could imagine and they were true. And carefully I broke off just one petal from the flower that Rayne had given me and I put it in the window with trembling fingers. So I would know where once we had lived when I was outside and far below; so I would remember that place for always. And I packed my rucksack and found the book in its hiding place.

I went downstairs and there was not a sound on the thirteenth floor as I passed the door, my breath held. And I went outside into the morning at last and looked up. I would not go until I had seen the petal.

Once I had left that place with the metal sign pointing to somewhere I simply could not decipher, the path ran straighter. The blind face of the great house lay behind me: I felt its presence yet. Strange how much strength that water seemed to give me, and as I walked I wondered if indeed it had been a spring. When I crouched to drink, I had feared it would taste muddy and bitter. I had no choice now but to rely on whatever water I was fortunate enough to stumble across, and much of that was set to be polluted and dirty. But this had been like no water I had tasted in long enough; it was sweeter and fresher by far than what had come from our taps in the city. It was like the well water we had once had at the cabin, the water I went for with a pail early in the morning. That is what I thought of when I drank this. And so I went on, refreshed.

The path became straighter ahead of me almost at once. The shadows were lengthening; the day was closing in and the skies were a blue-grey, deep in banks of cloud, and yet not threatening. I reckoned I had a good hour of daylight left, perhaps a little more, though not much. It was then I saw the building over to the right. At first, in the dim light, I was not even sure it was a building at all. I thought it might be some barrow of ground, a low hill, and at that point it was still distant. I did not need to leave the path for it was leading in that direction. Then everything became slower; I had to cross a wide stream and a fallen tree. I missed my footing on the far side and went down heavily, twisting one ankle. By the time I had started off once more it seemed much darker; the evening was coming fast now and I hobbled on, watching every step so as not to risk tripping again. Then all of a sudden the path turned sharply right and began leading straight towards the building, whatever it was.

I could only wonder if the metal sign had been pointing here, towards whatever this place might be. I stood on the threshold, my heart thudding, looking all about me. The door had been ripped from its hinges and every window shattered. All manner of obscenities had been sprayed in red paint on the walls and anything of value shattered on the floor. It was a church.

⊰⊱

I went inside and my feet crunched on fragments of broken glass. Carefully I started down into the empty darkness. All at once I remembered the big house I had passed only an hour before and wondered if this had been their private chapel. I had read of such things: chapels in the old days that belonged to estate houses.

When Gorwel had come and begun his preaching: Lisa and a thousand others had been set on fire by his sermons and had come out to places like this to desecrate them, leave them mutilated and ruinous and useless.

I walked and I looked about me; I padded forward as though there should still be a reverence for the place even though the stained glass windows were shattered and the altar broken. For despite everything there remained something that I could not capture or define, far less even prove existed. Behind the altar, whose stonework had been shattered by a rage of hammers and heavy implements, there were the remains of a fresco:

96

a perfect sky and hills; three crosses set alight in the last vestiges of the sunlight. The mob had not even been able to leave that be; they had tried to rubbish it with their scrawling and their black paint. I crouched down and brought my hand over what remained. And those were the words that ran and ran through my head: *they could not take everything away.* For somehow what was left had been rendered more beautiful still. All at once I thought of something, remembered what I was carrying. I took the bag from my shoulders and slowly took out the book. I set it down on the broken altar and opened it, but now the light was fading fast and my eyes could not have hoped to read the words. I rummaged about in the bottom of the rucksack and found a stump of white candle, and I set it beside the open book and lit it with a single precious match. If I leant very close to the page I could see sufficient to read, but only just. I leafed for the words I had thought of and now wanted to find. My finger followed them as I read aloud and read slowly, struggling and struggling to decipher them. I might have been a man close to blindness, having to reach out to touch the words first to make sure of them. But the silence held my voice like a chalice.

"Lay not up for yourselves treasures upon earth, where moth and rust doth corrupt, and where thieves break through and steal: But lay up for yourselves treasures in heaven, where neither moth nor rust doth corrupt, and where thieves do not break through nor steal: For where your treasure is, there will your heart be also."

I stopped and breathed and moved one hand on the broken altar; the candle flame flickered. I raised my eyes for a moment and found myself looking through one of the shattered windows. There was the blue-grey of the night sky, and set in it one single star. The light was pale; it was not one of those dead stars that crackled with the fire of a faceted diamond. It was a pearl; one frail pearl in the darkness.

"Therefore I say to you, Take no thought for your life, what ye shall eat, or what ye shall drink; nor yet for your body, what ye shall put on. Is not the life more than meat, and the life than raiment? Behold the fowls of the air: for they sow not, neither do they reap, nor gather into barns; yet your heavenly Father feedeth them. Are ye not much better than they? Which of you by taking thought can add one cubit unto his stature? And why take ye thought for raiment? Consider the lilies of the field, how they grow; they toil not, neither do they spin: And yet I say unto you, That even Solomon in all his glory was not arrayed like one of these."

I stopped and let the silence flow back and then I blew out the candle. I simply lay down, realizing I could be here—that this was a shelter. I was tired and sank into a deep sleep; the floor was hard against my shoulder but whenever I turned I fell asleep again almost at once. I had only one dream I remembered the following morning, but it was itself of broken fragments and made no sense. I was back at the wall with the fresco and my hand was on that beautiful place, that promised land. And I crept inside the broken picture, the broken wall, into that land. And I felt the beauty and the healing of it through the whole of me. And I heard the calling of birds.

The first thing that I found in the morning was Rayne's flower. I held it as I crouched there, stiff and sore, and the weak light filtered through the broken windows. Where had she made it? Was it something Lisa had found in the house where the child's parents were killed? Had she gone to her room to sweep up a few scattered things before they fled the place, never to return? Or had Lisa made it with her, that red tissue paper flower like a frail poppy? I twirled and twirled it in the dim light of the chapel and thought of the words I had found and read the night before. It was the broken windows that made me think this. Was God somehow more inside these walls than beyond them? I looked up as the first weak beams of yellow-gold melted out of the eastern skies and filled the place. No, they did not fill the place—they danced on the floor in the very middle of the chapel, for it was through one of the middle windows the light came.

And what brought the light to life was the dust: it was not the light that was dancing but the dust within it. Almost like some spectral figure that twirled and spun. The light changed a little all the time and so did the dance. It moved bit by bit across the chapel floor as the light changed beyond the distant clouds. And what came to me was that if the stained glass windows were not broken, it would not have happened like this at all.

I was not sure what that left me. In my mind were a myriad broken pieces of thought, and I did not know what to do with them. I could see how they *might* fit together, but was that the only way? And then the sun was gone, snuffed out. It was as though I came to and remembered my thirst. I put the book down in my bag and I thought of the water I had found the previous evening. It was going back before going forwards, but it was the sweetest water I had ever tasted. I hobbled out into the morning, slow and sore and helpless.

I went back and I drank until I could drink no more. And it came to me as I crouched there that perhaps all three places were linked: the great house, the chapel, and the spring. Or perhaps at least the last two. Back before there were even such things as churches or stained glass windows there had been springs that the first people considered holy, sacred.

They had gone to them on certain days with their diseased and their dying, long before the church came and bestowed on such places saints' names, painted their holy gold over the bare ground. But what could be purer and more made of magic than fresh, clear water bubbling and running from the very heart of the earth? Perhaps they had been right, that there was healing; maybe it was true that wonderful things glinted in the water and did heal. The people who had come with their sledgehammers and their picks, they had not seen this. Something older than the bricks and mortar of the chapel, yet perhaps it was because of the spring that the chapel had come at all. Again I got up from the ground as though I had drunk more than water. I felt stronger, healed. For all that, I walked carefully back along the way I had come until I was close to the chapel. This time I did not turn to go there, but I stopped for just a second to look right nonetheless and remember. Then I went on, slowly and steadily, guarding what strength I had. All at once I broke out on a bigger path, a track, and ahead of me was a sign that had not gone, that was neither rusted nor disfigured. *Alumbria*. That was where the cabin was, that was where I was headed. I was going in the right direction. I could not be far now, but how far precisely I had no idea. At the end of the name Alumbria there had once been a figure, however long ago. That was long gone; only one edge of whatever number had been there now survived, and that was insufficient to guess what else had been there. But I knew I had to be getting close. As I stood there the wind rose and shingled the trees. The clouds were gathering: I had to keep going. I started along the new path as the first drops of rain began pattering in the trees on every side.

After half an hour the rain became a great deal heavier. It must only have been about eleven in the morning but the skies were so grey and dark it felt more like early evening. The path was leading uphill and in time it became akin to the bed of a stream. I slipped and slithered my way up what felt an endless slope into the woods, cursing as I lost my footing time and time again. My ankle hurt from the fall the day before. In the end I decided any progress had become so slow that I might as well wait and shelter under the trees. I fought my way up into the dark of their shadow and stood there long enough, watching the skies as the armies of rain clouds drove over. I had never come this way before because my father had only ever taken the car. The main road he took had turned into a minor one that in turn had become little more than a long, slow bumping. I had loved that more than almost anything, for to me as a child it meant the prelude to two whole weeks in the woods. The city had been silenced and was gone: we had entered a place that was part of nature. But that road to reach the cabin had curled round first to the north of the city: it had come from a different direction entirely. I could *sense* that I was getting closer all the time, but I could not know that from any map. Then I changed my mind again: I was so wet that I might as well keep walking in the hope that I would get there reasonably soon. There was little point standing under the trees until I was frozen to the bone. I slid back down to the path and began fighting my way upwards once more. It had been my hope that the rain might have lessened even a little but I think I was deluding myself. And it was as if everything washed away: the light I had seen play in the chapel, the fresh water I had drunk early that morning.

All that counted now was being soaked through and cold, struggling even to keep my footing on this misery of a track. At last I reached a place where the track split into two: one arm led left along the hillside and the other turned right. My freezing hand stroked away the mud on the metal sign.

Alumbria lay to the right, and that was the direction I would have chosen, even if there had been no sign at all to guide me. Now the track was almost on the level but if it was possible the rain was falling even more heavily. The track was a grey-white line stretching almost straight ahead, and sky and trees and hills around it were gun-metal grey, melded with one another as though worn into one by the very rain. And suddenly it came to me that this was winter: all of this should have been snow. Once upon a time it would have been snow and now we had melted it to nothing more than rain. My father in his childhood had remembered the ice on the lake; perhaps it even had grown thick enough for him to walk on. Now it was gone. There was nothing more than the grief of the skies in a winter that was not winter any more; that never would be again.

The rain was so heavy that it streamed across my face and into my mouth. I drank mouthfuls of fresh water. But now my feet were soaked and every step was heavy; I felt the water in my shoes. Still I recognized nothing and nowhere, and still the clouds drove over the forests and never ended. I passed a place where the hillside had given way under the sheer weight of water above. The land was gashed and broken where a torrent of mud had forced its way through, gouging out a path through the woods, taking tree after tree with it. I stood and looked at the scar for a moment: I could not get any wetter. There was no sense in hurry now. And then at last I recognized things one by one. A certain path with a low wall beside it, and a red rock that I'd once put on top so I'd be sure to remember the way. The pine tree that had been struck by lightning and had lost one of its great limbs. And the lake itself—down in the trees to the right. The childhood place. There was the cabin and I cleared the dripping rain from my face as I looked almost with held breath to see if the windows were intact, if it had been left undamaged. It sat silent where it had done all these years and looked to be untouched, as I found the special hiding place and scrabbled with shaking hands to find the key.

The locking of the door behind me and the suddenness of silence. The only sound the many hands of the rain on the roof, like the thudding of a hundred drums. The cocoon of that inside world unlit, the shadows of half-forgotten things on every side: a pair of my father's shoes that glimmered still the colour of new-fallen horse chestnuts; an ancient coat of his behind a door, so dried-out it was like a kind of skin; a book on a table with lists of birds my father had seen on the lake and in the forest; a towel folded and smelling like mushrooms with damp; my room and the flowers in a vase that broke into dust at the touch of a single finger.

Rubbing the window and looking out on a little circle of the world, and there at the heart of it the lake. Crouching there and remembering, feeling the years fall slowly back into place. Hearing the voices of my mother and father, and yet not quite as they were before.

I sat there and cried; hunched into myself until my eyes felt red and empty. I cried because I had got there: I had kept my promise to my father and to Rayne. I took out her flower from my rucksack with trembling hands and I brought out the book. *I had done this.* And then I came to my senses at last and all at once I saw myself. I most likely did everything the wrong way round, but I took off all my clothes first and then I began to set the fire in the stove. And I breathed thanks to my father for having left dry wood in the basket: enough for a day and more of burning. *Always leave a fire for a stranger, for the stranger might well be yourself.* I heard him saying those words with a smile, crouched at the hearth, as at ten years old I watched him, before it was done and we had set off for the city and home once more. It was always the last thing he did and it had been the last thing he did in this place.

I waited until the first flames had taken and the wood was cracking and whining behind the little window of glass. Only then did I go, naked and freezing, to search for clothes in the shelves of the cupboards. They were musty and cold, but what mattered was they were dry.

It was that night I began to feel odd: that childhood sense of not being quite there at all; of looking in on the world as though from outside; of feeling wrapped in a kind of cotton wool and being always a little way from reality. I had made up a bed for myself with new sheets, for the old ones felt thick and damp. I even dried the new ones in front of the stove as the fire roared in its glowing behind the little window. I had looked in every cupboard and there was nothing to eat, not so much as a dried biscuit. I comforted myself with the thought there should be good water from the well, but there was little point wasting all the water that was falling around me all the same, and I left a large metal pan outside in the seemingly endless storm of rain. I started growing anxious about the cabin; my father had built it strongly enough, but who knew how the ground beneath might change in a new time, a new kind of winter.

What came to me first was the thought that I did not know if I was very hot or very cold. I was convinced the cabin *must* be hot, for it was a good stove and had been raging for three hours or more. I had no wish for it to go out, but nor did I want to burn my way through the basket of logs my father had left ready for the stranger. A shivering ran down my back; I knew I had got badly chilled and I dreaded what might come next. I had no food and no earthly idea how or where I might find any. Perhaps this was as far as I could go. I sat on the edge of the bed I had made for myself and tried to think what I needed, remember what I did have. I put a few more precious logs beside the stove so I could keep it burning through the hours of darkness. I set a candle beside the bed and the precious box of matches. I went and found a cupful of fresh water from the pan: that was how much had fallen already. I sat once more on the edge of the bed and forced myself to think as I shivered, as the whole of my upper body shook.

And then, it was as if I heard my mother's words after all this time: *Remember there are apples at the cabin, down in the basement. Don't forget they are there, when the time comes and you need them.*

I remembered when she spoke the words as she lay dying. I had not given them any thought at the time. I had been sure she was delirious by then, or so distant in her thinking that daily life and its detail were far beyond her. I sat there still for a moment, not sure after all if the words I had heard in my head were nothing less than wishful thinking—her wishful thinking. Then I got up just the same, though already I was feeling the ground unsteady beneath my feet. I recognized the signs well enough. I crouched for a moment in front of the stove and shook so badly I feared I might topple over. At least I had to go and see for myself, and I had to go now before I risked falling and dying a slow death there when I fell. My father had been so proud of that basement room: it was the place he loved more than anywhere else in the cabin. It was the place where he could play at being a carpenter.

"All those words of Jesus," he used to say, "brought from wood and planed and polished. You can tell he was a carpenter all right."

He didn't actually care for me going down those wooden steps to find him. I'd dance around him, chattering about everything and nothing, and he would do his best to endure me. But he wanted his peace. I loved the scent of the place and I loved it now again as I lifted what I always used to call the lid, the little hatch, to start climbing down the stairs. I held a candle in my left hand, so the right was still free to steady myself. For there was no natural light down there. I went slow step by slow step, watching and checking and wondering all the time. It felt truly cold now as I descended, though I could not trust my body's thermometer. And there was the great case in which my mother had kept stacks and stacks of glass jars of apples from the orchard. I could never remember the name of those jars: they were squat things with a rubber ring at the lid and a metal hook that was brought down firmly to seal each tight. They were still here, that was true, but were they not far too old to eat? I carried up as many as I could stack in my right hand. One of them fell as I climbed back up the staircase and splintered on the floor beneath, but it hardly mattered now. I came back up into the light.

Starving though I was, there was little I dared consume. I was ill already and I had little desire to make myself sicker. There was no Simon to go in search of now. The worst of it was that I did not know if one or two of the six jars I had carried up from the store really were as safe as they seemed. I decided in the end to try tiny morsels, and if I proved none the worse for them by the morning I would have a little more. The problem was that my mother had had no idea how long it was going to be before I came back to the cabin. How could she? In the end I left the jars outside by the pan that was still collecting the rainwater that fell no less heavily than before. I stood there for a second, looking out into the utter nothingness of the raining dark, shivering almost uncontrollably, and then pulled the door shut hard and locked it once more. Then I went and put one more log in the red hot chamber of the stove, crept into bed, and blew out the candle.

It was to be a long journey of a night. Waking and the world of my dreams washed into one. Sometimes it seemed that the cabin was bright and lit, and I was sure I could hear voices. I heard them and I even answered back; I had long talks and arguments with them or with myself. I was sure that I heard a knock at the outer door, and I called to whoever was there to come in. Then I waited and waited and there was nothing. I thought I heard thundering hooves in the woods and was convinced they must be deer, but then I sat up and knew it was nothing more than the rain on the roof. I had conversations with the dead: I knew they were not really there and yet they seemed close. *They were just underneath the floor:* that was the thought that came to me.

And all the time I wanted to know where Lisa and Rayne were. Rayne was playing a kind of hopscotch on the cabin floor and yet I knew somehow she was not there at all: I wanted and needed to know where she *really* was. And even under all my blankets I was cold and kept waking shivering. But I kept the stove lit through the night: I was determined that whatever happened it would not go out.

⮂

I must have gone to sleep early enough, by seven or eight. Or at least I must have begun wandering through fevered dreams before finally falling into deeper and more healing sleep. It was as though I was held and locked somewhere strange and deep. Perhaps part of me did not want to waken again at all. Yet I did, in the very middle of the night, and somehow I knew at once that the fever had left me, had burned out and was gone. I lay and listened and was aware only that a great deal of things had passed.

I knew without any shadow of doubt that Rayne was all right, and I felt sure too she had wanted me to know that. I could not have any way of knowing if they had left in some rocket in the end for R318; perhaps she and Lisa were simply safe with the group farther north, that there had been some other solution for them. But everything was all right, of that I felt certain.

And I was well, almost foolishly well despite my half-starved state. I felt clear and bright and beyond any state of fever. Now and again I heard the thud and whine of the fire from the other room; it had calmed but had not gone out. I got up first of all, slowly and carefully, to do nothing more than put another log in the pale amber of the stove's chamber. I was not shivering at all now. And there was light in the room. I stopped, taken aback, not understanding. There was a skylight window in the ceiling of the main room; I remember my father telling me just what a labour that window had been. I looked up into it now and the full moon stared back at me, silver and pure and beautiful. The trees about it were still and the rain had gone. The night held its breath. I put two logs into the stove and I found myself getting dressed. My father and mother had left the cupboards well enough stocked with clothes; they had always done so, for sometimes they

105

would come here out of the blue, just for one night or a weekend, simply to be away from the city. I dressed in all the warmest things I could find and I brought my father's stick with me for steadiness. I stood in the porch in the end beside the full pan of rainwater and looked out over the valley. The moonlight brought all of it to life. I locked the cabin door and started up the track. There was one thing I had to do first.

<p>

I walked along the track to the little wood store that my father had built. Long before I got there I saw it had been broken into and what logs that had been stacked there pilfered. Why had they not gone on to find the cabin and smash their way in to find shelter? I stood there wondering. But I knew just the same that my father had prided himself on building a shelter on the edge of the woods that would withstand storm and strife. And he had prided himself too in making a shelter that was *carved into the very woods*. Those were the words he had used and they came back to me now: I had not thought of them for years. Not everything was gone; smaller logs and branches remained—they had only taken anything that had decent burning in it. I could hardly begrudge them that: poor souls hiding out in the dead woods until they had nothing more left.

The light was shining on the lake. For a second it looked as if it were frozen, and for a second I even thought it really was. I found the old path down the slope in front of the cabin and remembered a hundred different runs. Whenever we got there; whenever the last bumping of the car was done and my parents began unloading the boot, I had begged to be allowed to go to the lake. And my father's face had always said yes; he had not uttered a single word but his face had said yes. And I had run there; I always had to run. There was no risk of running now; the most I could hope to do was totter down that path like an old man. Trees had fallen or simply died where they stood: the wood was contaminated. Like everything else it was sick or dying: the sky, the earth, the sea. Once upon a time it had been a place of scuttling and whispering and rustling: soon it would be made of nothing more than dry bones. The trees were dying and they would be the last to die.

I came down at last, slow and careful, to the shore of the lake where once I had played for so many hours. And there was no ice and no winter.

Instead there were huge drums that had been dumped here, that had dribbled out their foul chemicals into the water.

⤎

I remembered the times I had swum here, had explored every hollow and ridge. Now I could not take my eyes from these drums that lay toppled drunkenly in the shallows, still leaking something yellow the colour of sickness. *Trepidol* was the name rusted away on the side of one of the drums. I had crouched down to look at them and I got up once more to start walking round to the far side. Before I had got halfway I stopped in my tracks and involuntarily crouched down: I was sure there had been the flash of a light.

I half-crouched behind a bush and peered out over the opposite shore, searching. The light came again and I flinched. My eyes looked again and then saw something on top of a small hill above the far shore. It was still alive: its yellow light blinked every four or five seconds like some mad automatic eye. Perhaps it had been dumped here at the same time as the drums. A warning light that had lost its mind, that no longer knew why it came on and went dark, came on and went dark. And there was no one left to switch it off.

Then at last I came round the curve of the hillside to the place where my mother had planted the apple trees so long ago. It was my father who had cut down the other trees first, the pines that stood in the way, to clear and prepare the ground. As though both of them had poured themselves, their love, into that poor soil. And the new trees had grown; they had climbed into the light. My father had even protected their trunks from the deer, knowing all too well that otherwise they would just be found and devoured. He had built little walls about the place, to protect the twelve trees. It had been an Eden. I went inside that little enclosure and heard my heart, partly because of the climb to the place and my weakened state, but it was more than that. I stood among the trees as I had done so many times before to pick apples, to bring back whole armfuls to my mother for winter. They were dead; the trees were black hands that looked as though they had been burned. And this is what came to me, that it was now nothing more than an *orcharred*. That is what it had become.

✑

And I stood there for a little time and looked all round. The dead eye of the moon shone down on the dead earth, and as I turned I understood something. I woke into a new understanding. That the earth and the skies and the seas were not dead, they were sleeping. What was dead was *us.* But that was not wrong; it was what had to be. For we had broken all of it and left it broken. There came a time when we had gone too far.

But long after we were gone and had stopped all we had done to poison, the earth and sea and sky would waken once more. Not everything would come back; there was much that was lost forever. But the very heartbeat of the earth, that was neither gone nor diminished. Deep its drum might lie, but beat once more it would. That was what I knew to be true, there on the little summit with its dead apple trees.

I started back to the cabin and I felt so light and thin it was as though my feet made no sound as they trod the path. I went back with one goal in my mind, determined to do one thing. But I could not go quickly because of my own frailty, and as I walked I saw the sticks of my arms. I did not know how I had lasted so long. I climbed back to the cabin, shaking, and the key struggled to fit the lock with my shaking. And when I got inside I went at once to find the book and I opened it. I thought how I had brought it back safe; that my father's gift had survived the long journey of the last years. And I did not feel afraid any longer.

"Also he sent forth a dove from him, to see if the waters were abated from off the face of the ground; But the dove found no rest for the sole of her foot, and she returned unto him into the ark, for the waters were on the face of the whole earth: then he put forth his hand, and took her, and pulled her in unto him into the ark. And he stayed yet other seven days; and again he sent forth the dove out of the ark; And the dove came in to him in the evening; and, lo, in her mouth was an olive leaf pluckt off: so Noah knew that the waters were abated from off the earth."

I looked up and out through the window, and the moonlight upon it was soft and silver. And there were white birds in the sky above; I heard their voices, for they were the song swans. They were coming back to the water; they were returning to the lake. And I went running and running to find them.

www.ingramcontent.com/pod-product-compliance
Lightning Source LLC
Chambersburg PA
CBHW030133260626
47156CB00008B/2932